LION TAMER

a Charlemagne file

K.A. Bachus

Cover by Marigold Faith

CHARLEMAGNE FILE TIMELINES

Short Story Collection
A Lighter Shade of Night,
mid 60s to early 70s

Novels
Trinity Icon, early 70s
Cetus Wedge, early 80s
Brevet Wedge, nine months later
Lion Tamer, five months later
State of Nature, early 90s
Vory, a year later
Swallow, five weeks later
Quiet Move, late 90s
Goat Rope, 1999

CONTENTS

PROLOGUE

B uddy faced a dozen of his most senior agents arranged around the conference room table in the SCIF. He had an announcement.

"I just sent The Woman off to the UK on a Charlemagne op that the Brits are hosting."

The reaction was as expected: stunned silence followed by loud sputtering and a few bangs on the conference table. Buddy raised his hand for silence.

"She is, and has been, our senior officer and has earned the assignment."

"She doesn't even have a coin," squealed one man with an unfortunate tendency to squeak.

"Now Squeaky," said Buddy, "that's not true. She has a coin, and she produces it on occasion. That time you paid for everybody's drink when she should have shared the tab because she also didn't have it with her is your fault entirely. It's not her fault you let her get away with it."

"But Bear hates her," said somebody else.

"Bear doesn't hate her, Sturgeon."

"He hates his nickname, and she gave it to him," said another.

"You hate yours, Cod, and that's as it should be. The whole point of our nicknames is to bring us down a peg."

"But Bear might kill her now that he's operational," squeaked Squeaky. "And what about Charlemagne? What if they rape her or something?"

Buddy's round, bulging eyes gave the stare this question deserved.

"You know them better than anybody, Buddy," said Sturgeon. "You were their babysitter for twenty years. You know what they're capable of. It's common knowledge."

"No, it's not common. Nor is it knowledge. I've never known them to be capable of what you're suggesting, and as you say, I am the person in the best position to have such knowledge."

Buddy did not share with them his private concern that she was more likely to get her throat cut.

ONE

My game name for that op was Barbara Kemp. I loved Barbara from the minute I learned her legend. A successful businesswoman from New York. That's me. Well, successful government hack from Virginia is more accurate, but close enough. I paid for an upgrade on my government-bought trans-Atlantic ticket just to celebrate. The bubbly was delightful, and so was dinner, complete with soft music and no turbulence. My neighbors did not bug me, so even though I did not sleep, I was fresh as an alpha mare when I arrived at Heathrow ready to break a few more glass ceilings.

The guy who met me at arrivals stood half a head shorter than me. As usual. He glowered at my left earring.

"Is it far?" I asked the top of his sparsely planted head.

"Not far, Love." He pronounced it *lurve*.

I'm not your *lurve*, I told him silently, nor your love.

"Will you brief me during the drive then?" I asked aloud.

"We'll see."

We'll see you pounded into the nearest ditch, Elmer.

I sensed the beginning of a strained professional relationship between me and this bona fide pain in the ass with the Oxbridge accent.

The luxury of my new position just didn't quit. Shorty here led me to a Jaguar. I settled into the leather passenger seat on the wrong side and watched the February rain in the headlights as we negotiated an endless series of round-abouts.

"Are you going to tell me about it or not?" I asked after an enthralling fifteen minutes of watching the windshield wipers make their rounds, or should that be straights?

Nigel, as he introduced himself after I demanded the name he was using more than a few times, took his time with an answer to my repeated questions. He used 'um' and 'now then' as parentheses around every phrase, but finally summed it all up with, "We'll have to see if they will accept you."

I pushed an escaping pin back into the hair gathered be-hind my head, careful not to damage any strands. After all, it represented a lifetime of growth. At thirty-eight, I still had no grey in the bitter dark chocolate color, and it reached to my waist. I kept it pinned up during business hours.

"They asked for me," I said.

"They asked for an American babysitter."

"That would be me."

More ums. Then a "Ye-es, well."

Nigel, I thought, you should meet the guys in my section back in Virginia. You have a lot in common. For one thing, you take up a lot of space—in that seat and on the job. Just like they do. I had to maintain perfection to claw my way to this peak, but you've been here what? Fifteen years? Not running five miles a day and living on carrots and spinach salad all that time I see. I wonder how you would fare against me in a marathon? No, I don't wonder. I'd beat you by hours, not minutes, but it wouldn't make a difference. They'd still pick you over me.

I examined his puffy face under the motorway lights. Small eyes, reddish nose. Diet soda was not his tipple.

"So you don't think they'll accept a woman babysitter," I said, stating the usual.

"Have you met them?"

Of course not. One does not go around seeking casual meetings with teams of specialists. One works with them if that is one's job, and this was now my job. One works with the team assigned and only the team assigned, and again, now assigned to me. If one works very hard and saves countless impossible situations caused by incompetence all around and by a touch of psychopathic madness in the sec-ond-rate teams assigned to one, then, after twelve years of 'not the right time,' one can beg and plead and threaten civil rights lawsuits to gain promotion to the best team. The one now assigned to *me*. Then one will have the privilege of sit-ting in a Jaguar northbound on the A1 with an upper-class Englishman who affects a few working-class phrases but never got his nails dirty and doesn't think one will hack it with Charlemagne.

The name of my new team made me push in another pin self-consciously. I hoped I would hack it. I hoped I'd be given a chance to hack it. No, I decided, I would not be *given* a chance. I would have to take it.

"Do you happen to know anything about them?" he asked, dripping condescension.

"A little." I had read each dot of ink on every scrap in the section file. It amounted to a little.

"Well, it's all changed."

"What's changed?"

"The team. They've all changed."

"How?"

"It's hard to explain to somebody who hasn't met them."

"Try."

I braced myself for the usual lecture, hoping I could glean something useful. Let's see, he'll say, in my umpteen years of invaluable experience, during which time I was equally invaluable to superiors and subordinates alike, not to mention colleagues, oh, and let's not forget the team itself, I have found them to be …

"In the fifteen-plus years since I agreed to take on the Charlemagne account," he began.

Am I a prophet or what?

"I've had a great deal of experience with them," he continued. "I know how they work, the make-up of their personalities, and so on."

And on and on.

"This is one of the things you'll find that will accrue to you as you gain in experience with teams of this caliber." He would spell it 'calibre,' I suppose.

I peered straight ahead through my lowered eyebrows. That is how high I had rolled my eyes upward. I listened. I endured.

"As I was saying," he said, "one of the things that always struck me about these men—I must stress to you they are men, Barbara—quite traditional and somewhat old-fashioned, I must warn you. These men are closed. By that I mean they show us very little; the rest is carefully compartmentalized. Thus, we see only their killing sides, the human computers that make the plans, predict the outcomes, and kill the target. All a babysitter has to do, should do, is provide intelligence and logistics, not psychoanalysis and not bloody backup firepower like you lot allow your babysitters to do."

He was referring of course to Steve Donovan, now a member of the team he once babysat.

I felt Nigel staring at me.

"Please watch the road." I said it aloud. Sometimes safety is more important than tact.

"Ever been out with a team like that, Barbara?"

"Once or twice."

"Whatever milk toast team or solo you may have met, this time it's different. I doubt you're prepared, *lurve*."

I repressed an urge to pop him one. He was driving after all.

"So what's different this time?" I hoped he would just brief me and not return to Spy Studies 101. *Please, powers of the universe, make it so.*

His tone changed. It changed so much that I began to pay attention.

"This time," he said and then sighed. "This time, they are a mess. The compartments are gone, and everything is stewed in together. It's a bit uncomfortable, like sitting on a grenade without a pin."

"Can I have a for instance?"

"What a quaint expression. It must be American, I'd say. I must remember it."

I felt my hair loosen at the back of my head but did not allow myself to adjust the pins. Who knows what else may be so quaint that it stops him answering my questions?

He was concentrating. I could tell by the wrinkling on his brow and the way he ran his hand over the top of the steering wheel. It looked painful.

Finally, he said: "For example—excuse me for instance, as you say—between the tasks necessary to lay a trap for the target they keep themselves busy by beating each other to a pulp."

"All? All four?"

"The two older ones, Mack and Louis. The younger ones spend their time as referees. There is a bit of a dust-up every few hours."

"You're telling me there's a fundamental split within Charlemagne?"

"I'm telling you whatever information you may have had on them is obsolete. I suppose, in a way, it is a blessing for you because if they let you stay, you will not be any worse off than an experienced babysitter. At least, where understanding the team is concerned. But, then again, I sincerely hope you can run fast on those long legs, *lurve*, because I will not carry you when they detonate."

I'm not your lurve, mate.

I looked at him in the red glow from the dashboard and ignored the clump of hair falling down my back.

"So abort the operation if it's that bad," I said.

"We cannot. There is too much at stake."

TWO

Hello, Heathcliff, I thought, as I stood on the gravel driveway and gazed upon the edifice before me. There was a moon that night, playing its light over the swaying trees, the spattering rain, and the gothic pile of a house in front of us. The house and trees stood alone in a large expanse of flat fields. But this was not a moor. It was The Fens of East Anglia. The house was Georgian, a rectangle with straight lines and large sash windows symmetrically placed, two rows of three each on either side of a double door placed in the middle with a central window above it on the second floor. An extra wing had been attached on the left, set back from the facade.

The house was imposing to be sure, but also decaying. An overgrown garden surrounded it, covering its walls with tall weeds and vines and providing far too many hiding places. The windows were dark. Plywood covered some of them.

Dormer windows above the second floor suggested attic rooms and small ground-level windows announced a basement. The basement entrance was probably around the back affording an intruder yet another means of ingress. The driveway swept past the front of the house from left to right, turning left after the building and heading toward a decayed stable block surrounded by an overgrown copse. Talk about a hidey-hole heaven.

The house was too large to be easily secured. The team would inhabit only a few of the many rooms, leaving the others open to infiltration. The remote situation could be a plus, though. Any enemies approaching over the flat terrain would be seen and could be easily detected if there wasn't so much vegetation crowding the walls. But inspecting all those rooms every time we went out was going to be a pain in the ass. What was Nigel thinking? Give me a small, neat, isolation bunker with no windows any day or at least its nearest equivalent.

No ghosts of tragic heroines were likely to greet us as we crunched our way to the front door, only four men, heavily armed and, according to Nigel, strangely lunatic.

So much for romance.

We passed two cars as we walked up the drive. Both were pointed toward the road and I was reminded about this very basic security measure. I added Nigel's failure to do the same with the Jaguar to a growing list of reasons I did not trust him. Not that I thought he might be dirty, only incompetent.

The contradictory cars copied everything else in this operation, like the crumbling mansion and the bumbling babysitter. One car was the trademark Charlemagne sleek and shiny armored Mercedes that babysitters worldwide knew to obtain when the team was in town. The other was a heap of indeterminate color and make, shedding rust flakes into the gravel and threatening to disintegrate at the lightest touch.

We approached the door where Nigel commenced the Let-Us-In ritual.

We were greeted, if you can call it that, by Steve Donovan. He had been first my subordinate and then my immediate predecessor as babysitter of Charlemagne. Bad move, I had told the boss when he picked Steve over me. Men so hate it when a woman tells them 'I told you so,' but of course, I said those exact words to Buddy. Steve was inexperienced, unprincipled, and just a bit too violent himself. A babysitter should not have anger issues. Our job was to support and direct the team, not join them in their work.

Still, Steve had the most beautiful pair of liquid brown eyes I've ever seen on a man.

"Hello, Teddy Bear," I said when he opened the door.

He reddened. Steve never seemed to understand the effect he had on women. "Don't call me that," he mumbled between his teeth.

Nigel waited for me to go in.

"After you," I said.

"After you."

"No, no. I insist. You are, after all, my senior."

This had the desired effect. Nigel did not know what to do. He squeezed himself through the half-open door and stood in the hallway searching for a way to introduce me to somebody I already knew.

We stood in a long hall that reached to the back of the house. Twenty feet from the door a wide staircase on the right began its curving ascent to the second floor. A small table stood next to a coat rack against the wall on the left. Two worn oriental rugs lay end to end making a pathway along the side of the staircase.

"What the fuck is Frank thinking?" said my former colleague and failed babysitter Steve Donovan. "What the hell is he doing?"

"The right thing, for a change," I said. "I am the senior person in The Section, Steve. I have been for some time."

I wanted to add: I was senior when you were chosen over me, you bastard, and see where that got us all, you included. But I didn't say it.

"Fuck, Barb, not now. I give you twelve hours' life expectancy."

Nigel stood nodding in a corner with a poker up his butt.

"I wasn't aware that black ops require a penis," I said. Maybe it required being dickish, but the two don't always go together. Besides, I think he'd agree I was perfectly capable of that.

"Don't be crass, Barb," said Steve. "This is the fucking worst of all possible scenarios. We...."

By way of introduction to the worst of all possible scenarios, the Frenchman, whom the files sometimes referred to as Louis, flew backward through the open drawing room door in front of me and to my left, then across the hall, thumping into the wall beside me on my right, breathless but still on his feet. He had been described to me so thoroughly that I knew immediately who he was, but descriptions are like pornography, just never enough when the real thing is required. So I wasn't prepared for the real thing. I reacted strangely. Physically. Not to unduly belabor the analogy, I kinda got a little warm.

At that moment, though, there was not a whole lot physically to recommend the team's chief marksman and gadget expert. Somebody had rearranged his perfect face. There was quite a lot of bruising under his eyes, suggesting the broken nose might be recent. The various regions of his black hair with its sprinkling of silver at the temples followed different travel agendas, and a scruffy beard sprouted unattractively. But the eyes. Black and wild and wickedly sexy. Plus, did I mention he was French?

He shoved himself off the wall and toward the door he had come through. Steve moved fast. He hit Louis squarely in the chest with the heels of both hands, forcing him back up against the wall.

In one of my more boneheaded moves of all time, I covered my weapon. What was I thinking? That everybody was armed to the teeth, check. That emotions were running high, as in outer space high, check. That all by myself I was going to play peacekeeper with my dainty little nine-millimeter, check. It doesn't get more stupid than that last item.

A stream of language flew back and forth through the doorway. Four voices, using French, German, and English. I understood all the words, but little of what they meant. There was an older German voice in the other room. That will be Mack, I thought. He was the legendary leader of the team, a mind reader with flawless—though deadly—judgment. Also, he was purported to be very good with a knife. Funny how we use words like good. A younger voice shouted across the door to Steve in American English. Must be Mack's son, the one The Section had dubbed Charlie. And, of course, Louis was not shy with a lot of French words they don't teach you in school, all of them used in fresh, imaginative ways.

Charlie and Steve kept up a running dialogue aimed at keeping the two older men separate. I stood there, still stupidly keeping my hand on my gun.

The shouting died down eventually, but the emotional testosterone release had charged the atmosphere. It would be unwise to light a match in here, I thought. So Nigel did just that. Imbecile. Even more than I was at the moment. Together we became imbecile squared. What a team.

First, he tried soothing words. Not surprisingly, a general atmosphere of 'shut the fuck up' swallowed that attempt. Then he hit on a new tactic. I acknowledge my part in this. I know my hand had no business being where it was, but really Nigel? Your dick is so small you have to play the big man by getting me fucking killed? I'm still a little emotional about it.

"This is your new American babysitter," he said to no one in particular. "Can you believe they had the nerve to send a bird?"

And I stood there with my hand still on my weapon. But only for about a nanosecond more. In that time, my weapon hit the floor and my body found the wall behind me. Louis had shrugged off Steve like a down quilt on Sunday morning. I can't say I stood against the wall. It was more a case of trying to become part of it because the man twisting my wrist and crushing my ribs was forcing the barrel of his gun down my throat by way of the underside of my chin, making impossible any verbal arguments I might want to make, like please, please, please let me live. With my toes barely touching the floor, we stood nose to broken nose. He had not washed in some time. Louis twisted my wrist a little bit more and a treacherous tear escaped one corner of my eye. The glee in his smile caused more treachery in my body and I shivered. I concluded that I no longer found him magnificent. Fancy that.

Steve picked himself up from the floor saying, "Fuck. Fuck. Fuck." It had always been his favorite word to use in any sentence or as in this case, as a sentence in itself.

A new presence—I was sure it was Mack—said, "Let her go."

"She threatened me. I will shoot her."

Steve's twelve-hour prediction was looking generous.

"Do as you wish."

This was unwelcome.

But it turned out to be open sesame. I was on the floor the next second, trying to hold my ribs together but still alive. As he walked away, Louis kicked me in the kidney saying *Americaine* in a way that sounded like an expletive.

The last to leave the hallway before me was Steve, looking mighty disheveled and disgusted. He caught my eye as I used the wall behind me to force myself to a standing position. I told you so, said his teddy bear eyes.

"Oh, shut up," I said aloud.

I picked up and holstered my weapon, then followed him into the drawing room.

THREE

"A woman is not acceptable," said Mack. I stood there feeling less like a woman and more like a cartoon cat, gangly, speechless, and with bits of hair sticking out all over. The large room we were in also had seen better days. Stained and torn upholstered chairs occupied odd places without arrangement or even consistent purpose. I counted three equally sad, shabby sofas turned in random directions, one facing and another perpendicular to separate fireplaces and a third slumped diagonally on three legs It seemed to have no function other than as an obstacle to movement. Springs poked out in uncomfortable places on all three and most of the stuffed chairs.

Mack looked about the same as the other members of the team. The little bit of grey at his temples was not as noticeable as Louis's because it mixed well with his blond hair. He had not shaved in days. His shirt was a wrinkled mess, but his holster and the SIG Sauer it contained gleamed. Come to think of it, all their weapons were pristine. Mack's tired blue eyes x-rayed my soul, surveying me as I surveyed the room. I had read his file a million times. He read my mind a million and one. It took me years. It took him a mere instant. He never blinked, only regarded me with terrifying intensity.

I croaked out my reply to his statement.

"I'm experienced." True. "I'm competent." We won't mention the incident in the hall just now. "I'm all that's available." Ah, now there's the essential point.

"Then we will do without," said Mack. "Nigel, take her home."

"Touch me and I'll flatten you, Nigel, you twit." Nigel quelled. I stood a little taller, deluding myself that I could handle anything.

"You need me," I told Mack.

An incredulous snort came from the Frenchman leaning against a high mantelpiece a few feet away. He picked up a fireplace poker and drew figures in the cold ash.

It was the briefest of distractions, so I did not notice when Mack produced his knife. He was that fast. Or I was seriously off my game. Or both. Probably.

The knife filled my worldview, so to speak. Or its edge did. That edge was fine satin, but I could see my reflection in the polished base. Mack's eyes were almost even with mine, but I felt like I was looking up.

"Leave," he said.

"No."

"You can do nothing here. This is beyond reason."

"That's where I do my best work. In Crazyville."

The satin edge receded. I saw a wavelet of doubt on his face; I let him see a tsunami of relief on mine. No use trying to hide what he can see anyway. Maybe he appreciated the honesty. He grew a half smile.

"Try," he said.

I turned to Louis, still keeping a third eye on Mack and ignoring the three spectators who had morphed into disinterested toad lumps. Wait. Was that a glimmer of malicious hopefulness in Nigel?

"Get some rest," I told the Frenchman. "You have last watch. I'll wake you when it's your turn."

"I set the watches," said Mack.

"No. I do. You have enough to do." Bravely said, considering I had no idea what he was doing here at all, besides beating up his best friend.

"Get some sleep," I said again to Louis.

He took two steps toward me, raising the poker and pointing it at me, his tongue between his teeth, lips curved in a wicked half smile. I did not flinch. He put the poker tip through the space in my blouse left gaping by buttons that had gone missing during our recent get-acquainted session in the hallway. A reminder, I supposed. He drew a horizontal line in cold ash across the ribs just below my bra.

"I do not take orders from women," he said, his eyes hooded.

"I'm not giving orders," I said, purring. "I'm just reminding you of what's good for you. That's what women are for. Now go lie down."

"Come lie down with me. That is what women are for."

Once again the all-mighty dick must be irresistible to women no matter how squalid its package.

But I digress. I had a job to do.

"I'd love to, Baby," I said, "but you need sleep first." *And a fucking bath.*

I wisely left that last sentiment unspoken.

He gave me plenty of time to get out of the way when he threw the poker at me. He gave me time so I could duck, so I could bow to his superiorness. He slammed the hall door behind him.

I did not crow like I wanted to until after Mack also followed my suggestion to get a few winks at the opposite end of the house. I didn't crow at all, though it was my greatest ever victory because I foolishly thought I'd wait until the others congratulated me.

Still waiting.

"I don't like this at all," said Steve. "He's never pulled his knife just to threaten somebody right off the bat."

"I suppose we'll have to brief her. I suppose they'll let her stay," whined Nigel. He sent a beseeching look to Charlie, hoping for a negative.

Charlie nodded and I thrilled to the delicious taste of victory as that whiny little bastard Nigel swallowed a helping of crow and began to brief me, Charlemagne's new American babysitter, on the operation his government had named SIEGE.

FOUR

Even though our mutual loathing was pretty plain to all observers, Nigel continued to call me his *lurve* as he unrolled his operation like a London fog. I wondered what he might call an actual lover. Sugarplum? Light of my life? I looked at his pudgy face, his thinning, almost ginger hair, and the few extra pounds he wore about the middle so that you could not see his belt buckle because of the overhang and wondered unkindly whether any woman would want to be called his sugarplum.

We sat at the coldest end of the drawing room, away from the other fireplace with its dying embers and extra degree Fahrenheit and near a second, boarded-up grate. This bit of desolation, if it were possible, made us even colder. Even spiders had refused to build on this depressing bit of real estate. No cobwebs decorated the grimy wooden boards. Despite a good-faith effort, the wood failed to stop tufts of dank air from invading down the chimney in a putrid miasma.

Steve and Charlie took the old leather sofa facing the door. Nigel and I faced them and each other from wingback armchairs. I caught myself pulling stuffing from the arm of my chair. Not a good idea to telegraph nervousness in this crowd. A small table between us held the obligatory perpetual coffee machine. Cozy, but like I said, fucking cold.

SIEGE, it turned out, was an elaborate trap laid for an IRA killer who was so deep his name had to be manufactured by Nigel's section. Cú Chulainn's hallmarks were small, surgical bombs—bomblets really—placed unerringly so they took out only a few bystanders along with the target. The press is part of the game and it seems that while a terrorist's agenda may require a few ritual sacrifices, too many dead innocents can be bad for business in some arenas, like Ireland. A collateral benefit to such careful sacrifice is that it tends to isolate future targets. Nobody fancies an unguarded stroll down the street with the Prime Minister, for example.

A thoroughly reprehensible character (Cú Chulainn, I mean), he well deserved to be an assassin's target himself, but his cover was so incredibly flawless there seemed no way in.

Until one day, he missed.

"How did he miss?" I asked.

"Target went to the loo at the last moment," said Nigel.

I shrugged. "Things go wrong in a big operation."

Nigel leaned forward in his chair. "We have word his next operation will be even bigger, and Cú Chulainn is determined it will not go wrong."

Steve got up for more coffee. "He has no choice. Miss your target once and your credibility goes to shit. Fail twice and you become a prime entree on this week's most lucrative assassination menu. If he doesn't want to be a fucking bulls-eye, he can't mess this one up."

"So what's the plan?" I asked.

I thought this was one of those obvious questions, totally in the context of the conversation and all that, so why did they go all tense and start throwing eyeballs at each other?

Charlie, as de facto leader in the absence of Daddy, broke the eyeball ping pong and spoke. "We began by asking what Cú Chulainn would want most."

A target who never needs to pee, I thought. I am pretty sure I did not say it out loud.

"We decided he'd want a target that does not move un-expectedly," said Charlie with a malevolent smile at me, "or a bomb that detonates only when the target is in range."

I suppressed a shudder at the like-father-like-son mind reading. Charlie is a young version of Mack, but more per-sonable, says his file. *Was Mack ever personable?* Charlie wears his blond hair a bit too long for these modern times, and his face is more mobile than his father's, so it is easy to think he might be more socially apt. Maybe. Or it could be just his youth.

"Louis designed a detonator that will work only when the target is close to it," he said. "So we put it out on the market and waited."

"How can a detonator do that?" I asked.

"Voiceprints."

"Brilliant. But that would require a sample and a real-time program, and…."

"Darling," Nigel interrupted, "the next target is most likely to be very prominent. Plenty of recorded samples in the public domain."

"I'm not your darling," I snapped, "nor your *lurve*."

He looked away first. There was an uncomfortable silence as I extended my stare for just a little longer.

"What if the target takes a vow of silence at the wrong moment?" I asked.

"That's Cú Chulainn's problem," said Steve. "And anyway, the target's a politician."

I smiled at the joke, "Why not just use a radio?"

"Range and interference become big problems when security is as good as it is with somebody that prominent. Also, we're talking big city environments, obstacles, competing radio traffic, and unexpected passersby."

"What about the programming?" I asked Charlie.

"We're offering the programmer as part of the package."

"Cú Chulainn will never buy the Frenchman." I said it to myself, mostly.

"No kidding," said Nigel.

"Sarcasm does not become you," I snapped.

"That's why we began shopping for a dangle," said Charlie, sticking to the topic, bless him. Was there a note of caution in his voice? He shook a clump of bright blond hair off his forehead. Definitely being cautious.

"We figured it would be a very long time before Cú Chulainn would deal with an Englishman, so that was out."

"And it had to be somebody credible," said Steve. "Somebody who could have invented it."

"We figured we would let the trail lead to the dangle," said Charlie, "and substitute Steve as the seller once we had a nibble."

Why were they both evading eye contact with me while explaining way too much? What the hell were they up to? *Oh, what have you done boys?*

"So did you find your dangle?" I asked aloud.

That stone fell down a deep well as the three men looked at me.

Nigel spoke. "We found an American lieutenant colonel near here at RAF Alconbury. Avionics engineer and commander of a maintenance squadron." He was very proud of this. Smug, even.

"And you want me to get approval for you to use an American citizen as a dangle," I said. Not so bad, I thought. Easy procedure. The answer probably would be no, but Santa can't stuff everything down that chimney.

"What's his name?"

"Diane Rutherford," said Steve, "and we're already using her."

Nigel gave me a gotcha look, like a woman as sacrifice was somehow new. I had no time for the toad, being preoccupied with the news that she was already in play.

"How committed is she?" I asked.

"Totally," said Charlie.

I find fuffing with my hair a great way to hide stress. Nothing like taming waist-long hair to create a pause and give you time to think. It also annoys the men, something I rather enjoyed doing just then.

I slid the last pin into place and looked up into those light blue eyes of Charlie's.

"There's no hope for her?" I said, forcing the obvious into a question just for the sake of a little hope.

"No."

I took a moment more to stare at him. His answering stare sent a shiver through me. So much for the illusion of affability in junior here. I looked away first.

"We let a few advertisements lead to her and then put some light touches on her home and office," Charlie resumed. "Both are on the air base."

"It wasn't easy, I can tell you," whined Nigel. "Her people sweep her office periodically, so we had to touch the sweepers as well. I could have used some cooperation from your people, but I don't know the resident here and to find out, I'd have to go through my channels, and…."

"And once you did, the whole world would know," I said, nodding.

He glared at me. Security breaches are a sensitive subject in the land of Burgess and Philby, not that we haven't had our fair share of disastrous treachery.

Their touch was just enough to reveal any new contacts. A full day into the op and three days before I arrived, a new man entered the dangle's sphere. He was an Irishman calling himself Keegan Teague. Charlemagne found him interesting and from that time conducted all the surveillance themselves. Nigel's people were very good, but not always sufficiently subtle for an op this delicate.

It took an exhausting and painstaking two days before they saw the first sign of tradecraft in Mr. Teague. He insured himself against a tail on the way to his work the morning before my arrival.

"Is he Cú Chulainn, do you think?" I asked.

Charlie shook his head. "No. He's a cutout."

"Can you verify?"

"We put a very light touch on his car," said Steve. "He has a car phone. Yesterday our effort paid off. We heard one side of a phone call. The phone was secure but the car wasn't, and we heard him tell the unknown other party that Diane was the real deal. He asked for instructions."

Charlie was almost apologetic. But only almost. "We did not expect verification to take so long," he said. "If we try to substitute Steve now, Cú Chulainn will spook. We can't risk it."

"So Rutherford is in to stay," I said. "Does she know?"

The answer was no and that's what we need you for. And oh, by the way, don't tell her too much. We don't want her so nervous that she blows the op, just cooperative enough within the strict bounds of need to know. That is, she doesn't need to know her likely outcome. You could appeal to her patriotism. She is military after all.

But this is a British operation, I pointed out to Nigel. Allies, he replied, cousins even. Then he called on my care and concern for my newly appointed team of killers, as I am so anxious to be an equal in this field of men, yada yada. I am also responsible for the safety of American citizens, I told him. I can't just push one blindly into danger without approval from a higher pay grade and I'm not likely to get that.

"Why can't she just take their money, hand over the device, and leave?" I asked. "Is Cú Chulainn in the habit of killing all his suppliers? How long could he operate with that business plan?"

Nigel rolled his eyes to contemplate the ceiling, but Charlie enlightened me. His taut patience seemed a tad condescending, but the words were clear.

"We want Cú Chulainn, not a cut-out. Because his security is above average, well above average—perfect, you might say—it follows that he must be the only one who knows his target right up until the last possible moment. By using a voiceprint to arm the detonator, a voiceprint that is to be programmed into the device by an expert, we force Cú Chulainn's presence at the sale. When the lieutenant colonel hears the voice, she will know who the target is. She will die as soon as the test is shown to work. They cannot afford to do otherwise."

Tut, tut, *lurve*, was Nigel's answer. Just brief her briefly. Then set Steve up with a cover that will let him get in close enough to teach her the program. The team will do all they can for her.

I looked at the two members of the team in front of me. Even if there were a lot they could do, they did not look likely to do it. Both men were exhausted, worried, and pretty much empty of the milk of human kindness. Steve's rumpled coat was open, exposing the Beretta he now wore too easily under his left arm. Long ago, only last year, he had been a compassionate man. Some reports in the file hinted at the same quality in Charlie. There was no sign of it in either of them now. There may have been regret somewhere deep down, but the question was academic. As the trap had been set, there was little they could do about the doomed bait anyway.

Apparently, Nigel had no regrets, or his dislike of me overshadowed his humanity. I felt him generate a wave of glee at my position navigating a fast course between Scylla and Charybdis. But then, I might have been misled by my distaste for the portly little chauvinist prick.

"I'll have to think about it," I said, as I fixed a pin in my hair.

They did not like my answer. Their expressions told me clearly what my decision could cost me.

FIVE

"I hate to tell you this, Barb," said Steve.

This is the male version of 'no offense but…', which is common among women.

"Then don't," I said.

"Don't what?"

"Don't tell me. I wouldn't want to spoil your day."

He looked annoyed.

"You're not as good as you think you are, you know," he said.

Not having time for deep philosophical discussion, I ignored him and went about my business. Nigel had bugged out on some lame-ass excuse, leaving me with one hundred percent of the babysitter watch responsibility on *his* operation.

The team never allowed a babysitter to have sole watch, and though I had usurped scheduling authority from Mack, babysitter duties did not change, so I got to stay up late with my former colleague, old Teddy Bear. Despite his sobriquet, Steve was not a cuddly man. I never said he was when I nicknamed him. He just looked like he was, with big brown eyes, rather luxurious brown hair, and a melting expression.

I did a physical security check of the doors, of which there were too many, while he with the beautiful eyes gazed at the gadget console monitoring the perimeter sensors Louis set up, lighting up blips and dots in a visual language all its own.

"Why can't Louis brief Rutherford?" I asked when I came back into the room. "Why does it have to be you? I mean, isn't the whole thing his brainchild?"

"He's too well known to the IRA," said Steve. "They will be watching. I'm new, so not as conspicuous."

"Why don't you just brief me, then, and I'll brief her." A little straw grasping was worth a long shot, as the aphorisms say. Sometimes a lateral move in the game can pay off.

Steve looked at me for a long second, then turned back to the sensor console. He sat in a particularly decrepit armchair before the little table that held it. I sat in the chair across from him.

"Louis hasn't told me how yet," he said. "He won't until the last minute."

"Why not?"

"Because as soon as he does, Misha is going to kill him." He took a long pull on a mug of lukewarm coffee, then said, "And I'm going to help him do it."

"Misha? You call him Misha? You really are one of them?" The hard look in his soft eyes gave the necessary confirmation.

"So the Frenchman has done something inexcusable?" I asked.

Steve nodded.

"Well, are you going to tell me?"

"No. I'm not a good witness. I don't live at Vasily's Carpet."

"Where?"

"Vasily's Carpet. Where it happened," he sighed. "I don't live there."

"Where is Vasily's Carpet?" I was not surprised this question got me bupkis. "Is this a town, a village, a...."

"It's a place. Okay?"

He was more than irritated, which, given his new close relationship with 'Misha,' could be bad news for me. But I've never been known to back off when pressing on could merely get me killed.

"What sort of place? A house?"

"Ask Charlie."

Like that was going to be easy.

"Any ideas on how to get Rutherford away safely?" I asked, more as a way to change the subject than to elicit actual information.

He wrinkled his brow and scratched at his beard. It occurred to me that this was the first time he had examined the possibility. I found the thought disturbing. Saving innocent American lives once had been his occupation, too. He started to say something, then stopped.

"What?"

"Nothing." He shook his head.

I pondered the problem. "What if she delays?" I said. "Assuming you guys are right behind Cú Chulainn, you could...." I did not know how to finish this sentence.

Steve gave me a crooked smile. "You're asking for fucking surgery here? If this goes down at Teague's cottage, there won't be time. You might have noticed that the ground around here is flat. It's a former swamp, Barb, and Teague's place is as bare as a baby's ass. There's not even a few flowers to get in the way of the view. It'll be a fucking bullet hurricane in a small space." He handed me his coffee mug.

I stared back at him. I don't fetch coffee. Besides, before he joined Charlemagne, Steve had been my subordinate.

He smiled back at me with the merest hint of venom. He's been taking lessons from that fucking mind reader Mack, I thought. I took the mug. I had to make a new pot. It took some time to fetch and carry from the kitchen half a world away.

"You think it will be there, then?" I asked when I handed him the mug. "Teague's place, I mean."

He nodded. "The device will work on battery power once programmed, but it will need a computer for the programming, and that requires mains power. The cottage is perfect. It's a helluva lot better safehouse than this pile."

He had noticed the things I noticed, which meant the team knew Nigel's arrangements were not optimal. I wondered why they were putting up with it, but then they had a host of their own problems at the moment.

"About the only thing this place has going for it," Steve continued, "is that it's almost big enough to keep those two separated."

"Do you think Teague will be alone?" I asked, driving an idea from my head almost as soon as it was born.

He answered in his own way. "I'll do my best, Barb. We don't know how many there will be, but I'm pretty sure Teague's men won't be all that accommodating."

SIX

"You should cut your hair," said Charlie when he came on watch.

His own blond mop stood out in all directions.

"I bet you say that to all the girls," I said. "I haven't been so flattered since a bald, fat man in a wife-beater t-shirt wolf-whistled me."

His blue eyes stared through me with an expression a trifle too malignant for my taste.

We settled down in the drawing room after checking the perimeter and the sensors once again before sending Steve off to bed.

Charlie took a long sip of a tepid cup of coffee. It is a rule enacted by the universe of operational discomfort that coffee remains just over room temperature during any operation. That is, when there is coffee at all. Hot coffee must be discouraged. It would make us all comfortable and weak. At least, that's my theory. More likely it's a case of overworked coffee machines which must be completely dead before cheapskates in government offices will allow replacements. I've never been on an op with a recently replaced coffee pot but have often wondered what such a nirvana would be like.

Charlie wore the same shirt as earlier but had ditched the coat and tie. His Glock 17 was strapped under his arm. He was rumored to be almost as accurate with a firearm as Louis.

"You're too old for such long hair," he said.

"I was not aware there was a statute of limitations on hair length," I said. Hello pot, I wanted to say. He was young, but no teenager.

"Just trying to help."

"With …?" I raised one eyebrow.

"With Louis."

I had to run through the entire year-long five minutes of my earlier encounter with that particular deranged killer. Was he talking about my mock flirtation at the end?

"Are you talking about the little bit of flirting that helped get him to go upstairs?"

"You know I am."

"No, I don't know. I figured you were smart enough to recognize a bluff."

His blue eyes scanned my mind, even the parts I couldn't read myself. I felt myself blushing and all my attempts to squash it made it predictably worse. I'm sure my head looked like a beet with long hair, which is why I found us a new topic to talk about.

"So what is Vasily's Carpet?" I said, apropos of nothing.

If the topic shift puzzled him, he didn't show it. But he did take his sweet time answering.

"It's a carpet."

"Let me guess. It's a carpet that belonged to Vasily." Let's all join the smart aleck society, shall we? I left this part unsaid. I think it was his ability to be perfectly still that most unnerved me.

Vasily had been the bomb expert of the team for almost twenty years. He was killed eighteen months before this operation, just before Charlie joined the team.

"You think you're witty, but you're not, you know," he said.

I am ever so grateful for all the help I'm getting these days from the Barbara Kemp Improvement Coalition. Especially from those members who think they know what I think. I would have said this out loud, but I understood he was quite the expert with that Glock. The files were very clear on this point. Also, he was far too accurate in the freaky mind reading he must have learned from Dad.

"So Steve said it's a place. How is a carpet a place?" I asked. "I mean, other than for fleas."

"It is the name we have for the place where we live," he said. "Vasily spent much of his youth in various prisons. During an early operation in Beirut, he commissioned a carpet to cover the length of the hallway in one wing of our house. It is otherwise a barren hallway because of our security needs. The rest of the house is monitored, but there we have some privacy, with just a few very secure cipher locks, and no surveillance. Papa and Louis swore at him the whole way out of Lebanon as they lugged the carpet with them, but he would not leave it.

"My father knew Vasily's prison history made him very spartan because he did not decorate his rooms. But after they laid down the carpet, he realized even for Vasily a long hall with a locked door at the end was too stark. The carpet made our home into a Not Prison. So it is a place. It is our Not Prison."

This was way too much information. Was I, like Diane, also not expected to live?

"But Steve does not live there?"

"No, he doesn't. His wife Sally refuses, despite the risks."

"Is it not sufficiently 'Not Prison' for her?"

"No, I don't think so. It is a pleasant enough place. She objects to the other inhabitants." His half smile seemed a trifle sad, I thought.

"You have to be a bit of a lion tamer to share our cage," he continued. "And she is not." He smiled. "You are, though. That was a nice piece of work you did with those two earlier."

I basked in the compliment. "Thanks. Steve seems to think I'm not a good babysitter."

"I did not say you're a good babysitter, only that you did some nice work then. You succeeded with my father and Louis because you are a woman, not because you are especially competent. And maybe you have experience with a whip and a chair," he said with a crooked smile.

Welcome to my circus, I thought. What funny thoughts men get up to. I changed the direction of the conversation by posing the same question I had given Steve. Charlie thought about it and shrugged. He and Steve were becoming two of a kind.

"She is military," he said finally. "I presume she is prepared to give her life for her country." He stretched his arms behind his head and yawned.

"This op is not for her country," I said. "It's for Nigel's."

"Then why are you here?"

I was pretty sure he wasn't asking for an explanation involving the special relationship, so I rolled my eyes and waited.

With a sigh, he said, "Somebody would have to go in early—and all that, as Nigel would say. It would blow the op, but it's that or bye-bye Diane." He flicked his long fingers. I was suppressing a lot of shudders during this conversation, this one being the most challenging.

"Would the team do that?"

He shook his head. "Can't. We would never work again. It will be hard enough without Louis. You need to find another team."

Snowball in hell, and all that.

We settled into a companionable…. well, comfortable—make that careful—silence for a while, at least on my part. Charlie ignored me pointedly, but I was acutely aware of his presence. I checked all the entrances, the windows in all downstairs rooms, the locked door to an extremely creepy cellar, and the upstairs rooms not currently occupied by sleeping specialists. Another staircase—there were three in this house—led to an even creepier attic. I came down from there covered in cobwebs and told myself the feeling of things crawling up my leg was purely psychological.

Back in the drawing room, I sat down in one of the chairs by the fireplace still generating a wisp of heat, and lifted my pant leg to reassure myself that the crawly feeling was all in my mind. There was, indeed, a not very large spider at my ankle. I brushed it off with a shudder but knew enough not to shriek because I felt Charlie watching me. I could not afford to let him think I was some shrinking female who is afraid of spiders. I'm not. I am a shrieking female who is terrified of the creepy things. It was a close distinction in my mind, between Mack and his knife and the spider on my leg.

I looked up. Charlie was gazing first at me and then pointedly at his empty coffee mug. I wondered if he thought he could intimidate me into waiting on him. He would be wrong. I ignored him.

He snapped his fingers. I examined my nails. I never heard him and had no idea he was next to me until he picked up my hand, put his mug into it, and pointed to the coffee machine ten feet away.

I put the mug on a small table next to the chair and resumed looking at my nails. I have younger brothers. I'm good at this game, but Charlie cheats. He pinched the nerve at the base of my neck, the one my mother always made most effective use of.

"Ow! Cut it out. I'm not your servant."

He pulled me to my feet and grabbed an arm. I defended myself quite adroitly, but he had an even more clever move that landed me on my back and out of air. I rolled as I tried to breathe and tried to crawl out of his way, but he was sitting on top of me, pressing his advantage with his weight and an iron grip on my wrists. I was ready to use my legs to unseat him, but he anticipated the move, stretching out on top of the length of me, with his nearly equal length and stronger legs. He pinned my wrists to either side and grinned at me before he took full advantage in a way my brothers never did.

It was invasive, aggressive, and almost violent, and I knew I could not stop him, was trying to resign myself to it, to the ignominy of falling prey to this kid, when somebody said, "Charlie, cut it out. Your dad will be pissed if he finds out you're not watching the sensors."

Really, Steve? I wanted to shout at him. I'm down here in peril and you're worried about the fucking sensors? I couldn't say it though because Charlie still had his tongue in my mouth. I was tempted to bite down, but there was that Glock. He broke off the kiss in a leisurely way, nuzzled my ear, bit my neck, and said, "An opportunity must be seized, Steve. Do me a favor and watch the sensors for me."

"I'm not sitting here while you rape the babysitter."

"I am not raping her. She consented. She started it."

"Sure she did. Come on, get up. She has to go wake your dad and Louis. Which one should she wake first?"

But Charlie had resumed his ownership of my mouth, pinned both wrists in one hand above my head while the other unzipped my pants and began exploring inside them. I tried to struggle but was completely immobilized.

"I think she should wake your dad first," said Steve. "He will want to be up earlier."

"It's not rape, Steve. Who ever heard of a specialist raping a babysitter? She would not get me a cup of coffee. What use is a babysitter who won't get me a cup of coffee?"

"You know she used to be my boss. I'd prefer she not be damaged."

"Are you going to stop me?" With that, Charlie continued his campaign, sliding two fingers into me.

"I guess I'll go ahead and wake up Misha then, since the babysitter's busy." Steve stood up.

"Fuck, Steve." Charlie rolled off me, picked up his mug, and walked over to the coffee pot. "Louis is okay. It is my father who has gone off the deep end."

This was said with such nonchalance, one would think there was no woman on the floor picking up the pins dislodged from her hair.

"Okay? Louis is okay?" Maybe the incredulity in my voice had something to do with the memory of the dent

Louis's gun had made under my chin. The memory did not help to still the shaking of my hands as I buttoned my pants.

"I mean he is his usual self." Charlie looked down at me with a patient look on his face in such a way as to make it clear he was fast losing that commodity and I would be well advised not to accelerate the process.

He held out his hand to help me up. I hesitated with just a smidgen of distrust until I saw him become still, set his jaw, and give me that blue gaze. I took the offered hand. He nearly threw me onto my feet.

"His dossier says things like he is usually joking, jolly even," I said, trying to keep things businesslike.

Charlie took a sip of his coffee. "True. That part of him is gone. As it should be, given what he did. But it is my father who needs more sleep right now."

I was going to have to take his word for it, even though my stomach knotted at the prospect of waking the French-man alone and unaided.

"Will you be helping your father kill him after he shows Steve the program?"

"I have not decided yet."

"The jury's still out, then?"

"No. It's in. It is only a matter of sentencing."

"You don't agree he deserves death?"

"I just don't know if it's the best thing for the rest of us, but yes, he does deserve to die. I think that is pretty clear."

Charlie began a physical check of the doors and windows, leaving Steve at the console.

I was still shaking.

"He was probably just intimidating you, Barb," said Steve. "You can be a pain in the ass sometimes. It might help if you were a little bit more afraid of us. There is plenty of reason to be, you know." He looked at me with those deceptive brown eyes and I had difficulty keeping the fear down to just a little bit more.

I wondered about it as I climbed the stairs to the room where Louis was sleeping. I wondered what crime a professional killer could commit that his closest friends would find unforgivable.

SEVEN

I sang as I climbed the staircase. I don't remember the song, just that it gave me a few chances to belt out some notes, all of them happy, because happy is the order of the day—or night—when one is about to wake a specialist during an exhausting and dangerous operation in which his team has lost its fucking collective mind. I stood in a long hallway connecting the two symmetrical wings of the house and stopped at the door to a room where the Frenchman was presumably having sweet dreams. Taking cover at one side of the door, I knocked.

"Hello there!" I sang the greeting in the happiest voice I could muster.

No answer.

I swung the door open, still staying away from the opening.

Continual, creepy nothingness.

I peered inside, then followed my nose cautiously, keeping up a cheerful banter all the time.

The room was large, square, and very dim because its window was one of those that had been boarded up. Early daylight had to force itself through spaces between the boards. A double bed was pushed up against the wall opposite the door. Beside the bed stood a broken dresser. Two large wardrobes occupied either side of the door, leaving it pretty much indefensible. Despite all this dangerously positioned storage space, nobody had seen fit to use it. Bags and gear littered the floor. Clothing was heaped on the bed.

Also heaped on the bed, fully clothed, even wearing a loosened tie, lay Louis. His legs stretched their considerable length toward the door. He had flung his left arm over his brow obscuring his eyes in the uncertain light from the hallway. His right hand lay loosely on the weapon in the shoulder holster on his left side.

I was going to have to approach him. He was making sure of it. I gently wiggled the toe of his left shoe. "Rise and shine, *mon ami*. It's your watch."

No reply. Did his hand just now tense on the gun pulled halfway out of its holster?

"All right, Buster," I said in English. "I know you're awake. I'm not stupid and I'm not coming any closer. Get up."

I turned on my heel and stalked out the door, expecting a bullet in my back the whole way.

Because I survived, I was able to put on a fresh pot of coffee downstairs before he arrived. *Lucky me.* Louis and Charlie exchanged curt nods by way of shift change procedure, and the great ignoring began. We spent the first hour in silence.

Of course, I was the one making coffee. And where the hell was Nigel?

I sat on the three-legged purple sofa near the chair where Louis occupied himself with his gadgets while Steve raided the refrigerator in the kitchen. All the reports had described Louis as fastidious and expensively tailored. What I saw was flatulent and slovenly. Were the reports a lie? Charlie said he was still his real self. Was this his real self?

Maybe I was staring too much in horror, because just then he spoke to me, for the first time acknowledging my presence in the room.

"Do you use that bluff often?"

My mouth opened and closed again without anything at all coming out, let alone anything intelligent.

"I am wondering," he continued in a strange aristocratic French that I had not heard before in real life, "whether that was something you made up in another flash of idiocy, as when you put your hand on your weapon in my presence, or whether you have used it before and somehow survived the experience. Perhaps a witch doctor gave you a talisman to keep such things from blowing up in your face."

He looked at me while he drank his coffee.

I squawked "What …?" Then remembered the flirting tone I had used earlier to get the job done. It seemed to have these guys so, shall we say, exercised.

"What?" He screeched, mocking me. "What I am asking, Barbara," he said, leaning toward me, "is have you been raped on the job before? How many times?"

I got a D in Pokerface 101 at Spy University, so he saw my discomfort.

"So you are willing to risk it again?" he asked. "Maybe it was not so bad, eh?" He cocked his head and looked at me with narrowed eyes. "No," he said slowly. "Something has happened. Here. Now. Turn around."

To refuse would confirm his suspicions. I was a lot more than a little bit afraid now. I had thrown my hair back up under its guard of pins, but without a mirror or comb, it was tufted strangely. There was no help for it. I was more than a little disarranged.

When I faced him again, he said, "I wonder what Misha will say when he sees you. Perhaps he will say you wanted it."

Nothing like a nice hot shot of anger to help one find one's voice.

"Don't be ridiculous," I said. It wasn't as if I could say fuck you, which was my first choice. He might take me up on it. So I sounded like June Cleaver instead.

"I am never ridiculous." His black eyes studied my face. "Rape is a fear then, as it is for most people, even men. But it is not the best way to hurt you, eh? What is the best way, I wonder?"

If I knew the answer to that, I certainly was not about to enlighten him.

"So tell me what happened at Vasily's Carpet?" I said, by way of deflection.

"Who told you about Vasily's Carpet?"

"Charlie."

"But why you?" His brow wrinkled as if he were genuinely puzzled. "Maybe you remind him of his mother, eh?"

That was a creepier question than he knew. "You're saying I look like her?" Tidbits of gossip are part and parcel of intelligence work.

"No. She was very beautiful."

Your new nose doesn't exactly make you look like Adonis either, Sunshine. I pushed a pin back into my hair.

He regarded me steadily. "What else did Charlie say? Or … do?" He paused. "He has used your sex to intimidate you, has he not?"

"Another word for it is assault," I said, still seething.

"Any assault is an invasion of the body," said Louis, "but one that involves sex is more terrible because it is more intimate. How intimate was he, exactly?"

I did not want this conversation. No part of it was comfortable or comforting. But he would not leave it alone.

"Did he enter you?" he said.

I took a shuddering breath. "His fingers," I said. And his tongue, I might have added, but it was all of a parcel and no one detail felt less invasive than any other.

"Let me see," Louis speculated, "he immobilized you. You had no way to defend yourself. On the floor, perhaps?"

I stared at him open-mouthed with 'how?' unvoiced.

He smiled. "I know how he fights. After all, I am one of his teachers. His purpose was to intimidate, of course. Charlie does nothing without purpose, like his father. He was setting the parameters of his relationship with a new babysitter. You would do well to heed him."

"You're saying he's dangerous?"

Louis's eyebrows drew up in surprise. "We are all dangerous."

"But is he as dangerous as his father?"

"Oh, no. More dangerous. Much more dangerous."

"What did you do to make Mack so angry?" I said after a moment to deflect the conversation away from me. I needed to breathe again just a little.

It took him a minute to weigh his answer. "I raped his wife."

"Um, his wife is dead." I put my hands in my pockets so he could not see them shaking.

"He married again."

"Yeah, that would do it then. I can see why he's not taking it well."

"He says I betrayed him."

"Wait, she's raped but he's mad because it's about him?"

I got to see the wrinkled forehead again, but it didn't last long.

"I told him it was not about sex! I hated her! It was the best way to hurt her! You are right. It was not about him. I never thought about him."

"Never thought about your best friend and lifelong business partner? Okay. But why did you want to hurt her?"

Something broke or snapped or whatever you call it. Some reserve drained, past his teeth, into the air around my ears. It was a jumble. None of it seemed familiar because none of it came from the files back in The Section. Much of it I could not understand. Though I speak French fluently, his accent was so obscure I had difficulty with it at times, and I had no frame of reference for the things he was telling me.

"She has a problem with sex," he said.

"You said this was not about sex."

"Rape is about power, not sex. Her problem with sex made it the best way to hurt her. Why does nobody see this?"

"Presumably she's okay with sex in her marriage," I said, doubting that a man like Mack would take up celibacy even outside of marriage let alone with a wife.

Louis ignored this, which was probably a good thing. "That Chicago operation—she would not say, so we chose playing cards and Misha picked the ace and Vasily was disappointed. But again, there was our own Chicago op later, for revenge. We came home, and Vasily was dead, and Misha's wife and daughter were dead, and he wanted comfort, he said, and she gave him comfort. Like nobody else wanted comfort? I loved them all, too, of course. How could anyone not? So now they are married and Miss Holy Pureness …"

A pin made its way out of my hair before I could push it back. I looked at the man with the broken nose sitting before me. "You're right," I said. "It wasn't about Mack."

EIGHT

We spent the rest of our introductory alone time talking, even while we checked doors and windows and as Louis kept one eye on his precious sensors while I made pot after pot of coffee. The only thing we did not talk about was the op itself. There was also no more explanation of what had happened at Vasily's Carpet.

Despite that, I learned more than I could ever include in the file. For example, the original team members, Misha, Louis, and Vasily were distantly related and had grown up in each other's houses. Misha's family had raised Vasily, who gave Misha his name. Until then, he had been simply Michael. I heard about childhood squabbles with each other and with their siblings and the interference of nannies.

"Nannies? You guys had nannies?" I asked.

"Yes. Of course."

Doesn't everybody?

"I caused Misha's nanny to be fired," said Louis. "When I was four years old my older brother ruined my baby sister's christening blanket while playing with a bottle of ink. He blamed Misha. I tried to tell them he was innocent, but Misha's nanny could not speak French, so she decided he was guilty and should not have supper that day. Misha said it took him a long time to forgive me."

"Forgive you? What about your brother?"

"Misha was three. By the time he understood what happened, he and I had become good friends. Friends are easiest to blame and hardest to forgive."

"There is some truth in that," I said.

"When Misha's mother found out what happened, she fired the nanny and hired one who spoke French as well as German. I think Misha was bothered more by the loss of his nanny than by his unjust punishment. He did not like the new one. He connected the unwanted new nanny to my sister's christening and so to me."

During our second security check, we came to a small room off the kitchen where piles of tractor-feed computer paper had been stacked in a corner. These were the transcripts Nigel's people made of the various taps on Diane Rutherford's home, office, and life in general. Louis picked out a loose page and showed it to me.

"What is this?" I asked.

"The colonel's boyfriend wants a family. Look here." He pointed to a line about a third of the way down the page.

"I'm a warrior, Mace," Diane had said. I gathered Mace was the boyfriend. "No babies. No home. No two-car garage. I'm just not made that way. This is all there is for me. Sorry."

"This is all there is for me," Louis said, reading aloud.

I was beginning to like our doomed dangle. That is not a good thing in my business. I caught myself entertaining fantastic schemes, all at the last possible moment, refining the suggestions I had already gleaned and overestimating my heroic capabilities. Diane seemed a worthy object of rescue. I just didn't know how it could be done.

I looked at Louis, wondering.

"So you're a warrior," I said.

"Yes. I am the second son. First inherits, second fights, third son prays. I have a younger brother who is a priest."

"How did you find this particular conversation in all those piles of paper?" I asked. This was not something that would have been flagged by Nigel's bean counters.

"I read every word she says."

"So who is Mace?"

"A U-2 pilot on the base. His name is Mason Leupena. Keegan Teague's attentions have made the relationship difficult."

I did not want to revert to talking business, but the sun was almost up, and it was past time to wake everybody. We ended our house tour in the drawing room where Louis said something that made us both laugh.

Mack's scowl as he came through the door swallowed any weak joy that might have lingered in the room. He glared at Louis, who lifted an eyebrow in a dare. I occupied the excruciatingly uncomfortable space between them. I'm a pretty good fighter for my weight class, which is way outclassed by these guys, as I had discovered only a couple of hours before. I would have to intervene alone, without Steve or Charlie, and I would lose. Mack looked at me, turned, and stalked out of the room.

I followed him into the kitchen because I wanted to talk to him. I made him breakfast because I wanted to placate him. Well, that and I could not bear the massacre of half a dozen eggs being perpetrated by his hand as I closed the door behind me. What a mess. I wondered why Nigel had not hired help. It would be simple enough to vet people from among his own section's staff and just keep them in the house for the duration. They would have the necessary clearances and the place was certainly big enough. I filed it away as a future suggestion for Nigel, whenever he might decide to show up for work that day.

Now that the household was awake, everybody went about their own business. Louis conducted endless security checks, testing each sensor and tweaking its placement along the perimeter. Charlie stayed in the front room to watch those sensors. Steve spent the morning in the bathroom vomiting, mostly coffee. His ulcer was making him too sick to eat.

That left me alone with Mack. Not only was he up and awake, but his tie was straight, and he had shaved. His collar and cuffs were dirty, though. He carried his SIG in a shoulder holster. It and the holster were spotlessly clean.

"How about an omelette?" I asked. I tried to use an elbow as I took the pan from him. I am a fraction of an inch taller, and my elbows are pretty pointy, but I may as well have tried to move a tree. He glared at me.

"Sit down and I'll make you breakfast."

He sat.

"So how is your wife doing?" I said as kind of an ice-breaker. "This has to be a really tough time for her with you away and all." I looked over my shoulder at him sitting there as I whisked the eggs.

"It is not your business."

I noticed he had no timekeeping mannerisms. The table was populated by all kinds of clutter. Most people would at least push a plate away or pick up a saltshaker. The files had mentioned he was economical with movement, but this was on another plane entirely. He was economical because he was prepared to move in any direction, in any situation, at any time, and you knew looking at him, that he would reach that destination way before you. I suppressed a shiver. His blue, blue eyes told me he saw me do that, too.

"On the contrary," I said, admittedly with a bit of a squeak, "it is very much my business, or at least it is my job to keep the team whole and intact during an op. I've heard some disturbing things, disturbing for a woman to hear that is, and I would like to interfere as much as necessary and as little as possible at the same time, to find that sweet spot that would allow you guys to get your job done without any unnecessary, um, ah, unnecessary bloodshed."

Especially my own.

"Was your wife hurt badly?"I chopped up a bell pepper and cubed a bit of cheddar.

I gave him time, but nothing came. Just as I opened my mouth to continue this enthralling conversation, he spoke.

"She was not hurt."

"Physically? That's good," I said. "But, you know, there can be emotional damage in this situation. Has she been able to see a counselor?"

"No."

I turned from the cutting board. "She should see someone. The effects of such an event can be devastating. You must urge her to get help." I used my most sober, serious voice, and matched my face to it as I turned back to the chopped veg.

"She said she was not raped."

"Wait. What?" I spun around to look at him.

The royal blue eyes that normally held no emotion at all were not troubled in any way, but I could see a hint of confusion.

"She said it was only a kiss. She was not raped."

"Then, why?" I swept my arm through the air in a wide arc to encompass 'all this.'

"Louis says he did."

"And you believe the man rather than your wife?"

"She would protect him. And me. I believe him."

"Well, that's a first for the record books. Not only is a woman's word unbelievable when she claims rape, but now it's no good when she denies it?" I let my skepticism show a smidgen.

"Women have many strange reasons to lie," he said, not making my blood boil at all. "There are women who deny their husbands beat them. Their injuries are always caused by something else, often doorknobs and staircases."

"And men never lie?" I asked. "Louis could not be lying for some equally strange reason?"

Like a death wish.

Mack turned inward and was silent for what seemed like an hour, but after a minute said, or rather ordered, "Make the omelet."

After this interesting exchange, I tried a light banter, mostly about cooking, hoping to avoid any other touchy subjects, but he had used up all his stock of semi-polite conversation, probably for the year.

You could say we were charmingly domestic in a country farmhouse, with a well-stocked kitchen (okay, credit there to Nigel) and Nebraska cooking. I put plate after plate in front of him and he put away an omelette, hash browns, half a pound of sausage, breakfast biscuits, toast, and jam, thin buttered pancakes rolled in powdered sugar, and some leftover ham simmered in pineapple juice and brown sugar. The man could not cook, but he could eat. He was also a master of the insult. The language he used was incredibly clever, with layers of meaning, all of them hurtful.

He did not insult the food, though. Nor did he thank me for it, but I guess getting through an hour alone in his presence unscathed was thanks enough.

The clean-up was left to me, of course. I did not mind the lack of company as I stood before the sink, dead on my feet. Washing dishes requires little coherent thought, so I must have put my senses on hold.

In the middle of an op.

With Charlemagne.

This bit of choice boneheadedness might have eclipsed my introductory move in the hallway the day before. Either way, my brain was on idle, and I was enjoying the kitchen solitude when I turned from the sink into the chest of Louis. I had not heard him at all.

He lost no time. The pins popped out of my coiled braid and fell tinkling to the floor as he laced his fingers through my loosening hair and pulled my lips to his.

I am no blushing virgin. I work in a field populated by mostly attractive and very fit men, despite the few Nigels out there and I don't often say no. I might add that on occasion it may be my idea to initiate, and they also do not say no. But this kiss, this was new. It was an appetizer, the kind of appetizer that is a meal in itself and anticipates a more satisfying repast in the future. His tongue danced with mine but was absolutely in the lead, owning the territory of my mouth, exploring at will, conquering. It was an intrusion, impudent but not violent, more of a promise and an announcement of what was to come. The man had confessed to raping his best friend's wife. I knew what he was capable of, what he intended, and that I had no defense, not because he had taught that abominable kid how to fight, but because my body would not allow me to say no to such a man.

Hell, I'd have consented to lie across the kitchen table, but he broke off the kiss, looked at me with a slow smile, turned, and walked out the door.

I gathered what I could of my hairpins and my dignity and left the room looking like a scarecrow. A rather titillated scarecrow.

Nigel showed up just as I crossed the hallway. He stared. I tried not to look well kissed. He continued a steady regard and I almost saw him as he once must have been, before he became complacent and convinced of his male superiority.

I brought him up to date on the events of my over-long shift. Well, most of the events. I could see in his eyes that he already knew about that second kiss. Maybe it was the tangled mess of my hair, the look on my face, or his weak imitation of Mack in the mind-reading department. Or, it could be the mysterious male alertness to all things sexual in a woman. Pheromones, maybe, or other subtle cues that all men seem able to read, even gone to seed puddings like Nigel.

"I want to run something by you," he said. "Let's go somewhere we can talk."

My uh-oh radar powered up. We went outside into a grey, cold February day in England. I shivered. My hair hung in clumps; my eyes streamed with fatigue, and I was grasping my rescued hairpins too tightly in my left hand.

"I think we should team up," said Nigel.

"As in?" I asked. Surely not, I thought.

"As in we should work together on this plan I have been considering."

"That's what we're doing, isn't it?" I said with some relief. This did not have the feel of the usual opening line. "You know, the one where you decided to sacrifice a U.S. citizen to rid yourself of an IRA killer? Don't tell me you're only now putting in the considering part."

He scowled. "There's that, yes. But I think it would be good for both of us if we added a small modification."

"What modification?"

"We should keep the detonator. Think about it. If we could count on precision like that, and have it at our disposal, we wouldn't need specialists. At least not as often."

I knew, in my bones, he had something risky, probably deadly, up his sleeve. "The programming?" I said to throw a roadblock in his way.

He gave me an exasperated look. "Our lads are quite up to that sort of thing. Remember Enigma? And I'm sure my government would share it with yours, especially if you helped me obtain the thing."

I quelled my internal laughter ruthlessly. "Why not just buy it? Maybe the Frenchman would sell it to you."

He raised both eyebrows and said nothing.

"That's true," I said. "He would build in some weird ability to inform Charlemagne any time you did use it. How do you propose stealing it without them knowing you took it?"

More important but unspoken, without them killing you. I was beginning to think maybe Nigel was not incompetent; he was off his rocker.

"Have you seen them?" said Nigel. "Did you notice they are not exactly in top form these days?"

I did not point out that his lousy arrangements in this godforsaken broken-down, insecure safehouse were at least part of the problem. But tact and diplomacy are my middle names.

"I know this chap," he continued. "He's ex-SAS. He says he can get a few of his mates to help us. We should meet and put our heads together to come up with a plan. Are you heading to the base?" he asked, raising an eyebrow.

"After I sleep."

"Don't leave it too long. I'll call Stan and arrange a rendezvous when you get back."

I glared at him. I had not slept for twenty-five hours, in part because of his less than dedicated presence on the job, and now he wanted to throw me into some harebrained plot that would take my time, put the team—my team—further at risk, and destroy the mission. And those were best-case scenarios. Another thought flew out of my head before I could grasp it. I was too tired for anything but sweet dreams. Nigel was proposing a lunatic nightmare.

I climbed upstairs, found my way to the room that held my suitcase and threw myself on the bed. My eyes closed on a vision of the satin edge of the worst-case scenario. I was too tired even to shudder.

NINE

Two and a half hours later I found the Frenchman making coffee in the drawing room. We were alone, which I both did and did not want, but hey, it's a job.

"You didn't rape her," I said.

A pause. Then, "My nature is well documented in your files. Also in Nigel's files, in the files of many others."

"But you didn't rape Misha's wife."

The coffee machine hissed and Louis came toward me. He stopped a few feet away.

"Misha took her, you know."

"You said he married her."

"He did. But he took her first. In Chicago. She was the dangle."

There was, no doubt, more to this story. He had to be talking about an op that took place over a decade ago, another Chicago op before the most recent one. There was no dangle in CETUS WEDGE. Plenty of tragedy, but no dangle. I remembered an old op-rep, or operation report, my boss Frank had written. It was pretty bare bones as far as information went, sparing the reader such uninteresting details as who, what, when, where, and why.

"Was she as doomed as Diane?" I asked.

He nodded and looked away at my mention of the lieutenant colonel.

"She must have been younger than Diane," I said, "Frank mentioned a college student in his report."

He wore a stone mask and spoke in op-speak, terse and emotionless. "Twenty," he said. "A virgin. Misha took her." He gazed toward the coffee pot. It had begun to burble.

Hardly a parallel with Diane, aside from the fact that somehow the woman had lived to marry Mack. And there was a connection in Louis's mind.

"Did he rape her?" I asked.

He turned his head abruptly, looked at me, and frowned. "No. Of course not. She consented."

I was having difficulty with this conversation. None of it was in our files, but he seemed to think it was. Though he had mentioned a young woman involved in that op, Frank indicated nothing about her being a dangle.

"You said something about drawing cards," I prompted.

Louis sighed, distracted. The coffee machine began to spit. Soon it might reward us with the magic liquid. He certainly had an unholy fixation on it. He swept his hand through his unruly hair, sighed again, and said, "Vasily wanted her. He had her agreement, or he said he did, to provide what they wanted."

"They?"

"Ill Wind. The terrorists. They planned to bomb a tall building. I don't remember what they needed, another detonator, maybe. It's always a detonator. Technology is difficult to keep up with in this business. Expensive. No, I think that time it was a laser trigger, very expensive. We decided to dress her up as a tart and let them get part of what they needed from her."

"Part of the detonator or rather, trigger?"

"No. It was something they needed to buy the thing. A painting, I think. Part of it. It had parts to it. I think the coffee is ready."

He gave me a pointed look. God forbid an aristocratic male should pour his own coffee. But I needed this conversation to go on. It was pure gold and would make my career. What a coup! Besides, I needed to understand, to know what was going on, or there would be no operation, no career, and no Diane Rutherford.

I grabbed his mug from the coffee table, stepped to the machine, and poured. I did not pour one for me. The last thing I needed right now was to be interrupted by an urgent need to pee. It can interfere with the ability to listen.

"There were parts to the painting, you were saying," I prompted as I handed him the mug. The essential beverage was in that brief magical state of being hot and I was jealous. I knew the pot would be tepid by the time we finished this conversation. I felt very noble in my sacrifice of the ultimate luxury, a hot cup of coffee, in the acquisition of that boon of all boons, more information.

He sipped and nodded. "We gave her one part of the painting. We needed Ill Wind to stay busy trying to make her tell them what she did with the rest. To give us time to get in there."

"Did she tell them?"

He looked up, incredulous. "Of course not. She did not know. We did not tell her."

"And Vasily got her to agree to this?" I was demanding perfect stillness from the muscles in my face. So far, the team's concept of consent did not match mine.

"Yes, he liked her," said Louis. "He wanted her to live. If she gave them the whole painting, they would kill her right away. If they thought she knew where the rest was, they would press her, then kill her when they realized she did not know. Vasily did not want her to die."

What we do for love, I thought. She married Vasily and eventually Mack and was currently living at Vasily's Carpet, the Not Prison.

"So drawing cards?" I prompted again.

He rolled his eyes at my ignorance. "She was a virgin. Even worse. She considered sex, any sex at all, a sin. She had determined to hang onto it until old age, I think. She quaked at the sight of us. Well, not so much at Vasily. Maybe that is why he liked her. It was new to him. An innocent who did not fear him."

"So why was her virginity such a problem?"

Louis stared at me again, giving me too much attention. I gave myself an internal shut-the-fuck-up command because I needed him to stay in the past and keep talking.

"Innocents do not walk up to terrorists and hand them the means to blow up a building full of people," he said. "We gave her a legend to give her access. She was a tart after money, trying to sell them what they wanted. Stupid, venal, easy. Of course, they would check. Hell, Misha checked. And then they would know she was a dangle, and they would kill her before we could get to her. Do you understand?"

I nodded. Appalled.

"We all argued, but not Frank. He was not there. Eventually, Misha relented. He told Vasily to take her, but Vasily would not, so Misha told her to choose one of us. She refused. She had already agreed to the whole thing, but she would not sully herself in that way—or some such crap. We drew cards. Misha had the ace. He told her again, choose. She would not. Vasily was not happy, but I think he did not want to start with her that way. He wanted everything to be not what it was. Not Prison. Not babysitter's daughter. Not raped innocent. Not doomed dangle."

"Frank was not there," I said. "She was a twenty-year-old virgin with religious convictions, and you all played a card game with her to determine who would give her a plausible legend in a deadly op? And she consented?"

I thought my summary was pretty dead on. So did Louis, I think, because he squirmed a little, squinting one eye and letting out an elongated "*Ouiiiii*."

"And she is Frank's daughter? Is that why he didn't write any of this up?"

"No," he said, looking puzzled.

"You said she is a babysitter's daughter."

His eyebrows raised. I had given him information about our files and my boss.

"Not Frank," he said. "Fred. He was retired. I believe he was Frank's boss once, and I told you Frank was not there. He could not write what he did not know."

His lips curled upward in a crooked smile unsupported by the eyes he had fixed on mine. I wasn't sure this information made me safe. He finished his coffee, put the mug down, and stepped in front of me, not in kissing range, but close enough to reach my breast. He circled my left nipple, ever so lightly with one finger.

It's not as if this kind of thing never happened in this job. It did frequently. Normally, I would simply step away. Sometimes, I would slap the man, even if he were a crazy, beefed-up killer. Never did I allow myself to be demeaned like this. For the first time, I didn't feel demeaned. Nothing was normal on this op, and that included my response to this man.

"Your breathing has changed," he said with that slow smile. "You desire me as much as I desire you."

Charlie and Nigel came in then, following the scent of coffee.

TEN

As I drove the beater car to the air base, I spent twenty minutes considering all my options and the various bits of advice Steve and Demon Charlie had given me regarding Rutherford. I generated ideas, checking each one against reality and the odds. Fleeting thoughts of the past few hours came back to me, and I made a few tentative plans. None of these involved getting myself killed in Nigel's crazy scheme. There was something very wrong there. I would have to watch him.

I introduced myself to Lieutenant Colonel Rutherford in a bare room called a SCIF (pronounced skiff). The steel and acoustic countermeasures that encased the room were supposedly impenetrable by all the people in the world with Louis's skills. Having met Louis, I wondered and doubted just a bit.

The colonel had a firm handshake and straightforward gaze. A tall woman with long slim hands, she moved with natural grace and stood ramrod straight. She had green twinkly eyes and spoke with a low, fast voice that was somewhat breathless. Her short hair glowed with a too-even blonde color that I doubted was natural. I liked her and hated her immediately. We sat down at a large conference table in the room.

"Colonel, it is imperative...."

"Please, call me Diane."

I took a deep breath. I prefer my sacrificial lambs anonymous, thank you. I learned this important point as a child when a tiny yellow chick named Fluffy I raised for a 4H project grew into a surplus rooster and Sunday dinner. He was delicious but accompanied by tears.

"Diane, it is imperative you tell no one about this meeting or about the things we are going to discuss."

She nodded. I suppose she could not help the twinkliness of her eyes. Must have played hell with the people she commanded.

I told her just enough. I described Steve and told her he was a Hughes Aircraft technical representative, which was the cover I had managed to get him. *You're welcome, Nigel.* I explained that she should expect contact.

She nodded again, seemingly delighted with it all.

I did not tell her about the disintegrating Frenchman who doted on every word she had spoken in the last three days because of a niggling problem with the definition of consent, the man who would teach Steve what he in turn would relay to her in what I hoped would not be a disastrous game of telephone. I did not tell her about my intricate negotiations with a cold, knife-wielding specialist who had extracted my promise to fully cooperate with the odious

Nigel in return for Louis's continued life until the end of the operation. I also neglected to mention my deep reservations about Nigel's ability or even his desire to pull off the op at all, let alone without a lot of unnecessary blood, only partly because I couldn't mention Nigel or the true nature of the op at all.

Our conversation made me even more uneasy. Diane was so ... nice. She had an ephemeral quality that made you glad just to be in the same room with her.

"When I say it is important you not mention this to anyone," I insisted, "I include Mr. Teague. I can't say this strongly enough. It's important that you not mention this to him."

This was risky. I was disclosing that her activities, her life even, were closely watched, a breach of security protocol, but I had a feeling she did not take the situation entirely seriously. Maybe it was the twinkly eyes. Her almost playful manner made her someone I would be glad to go clubbing with, but we were not clubbing. We were discussing her possible—probable—death, though she did not know it. I wanted to tell her I was being as serious as a heart attack—her heart attack.

"Keegan?" she said. "Not Keegan! What has he done?"

"Just don't tell him any of this. He is likely to ask you about the device. Act like you are selling it. Let him make the arrangements. Steve will provide some protection for you."

Some. Right. Another breach. Was she getting any idea of the danger she was in? If she did, her perfect features did not say so.

"But I can't believe Keegan would be involved in anything like this," she said, chuckling. "Who'd have thought, huh?" An idea did occur and her brow furrowed. "He's not in any danger, is he?"

I was momentarily speechless. She was not catching on, though she was not stupid. I began a verbal tap dance. Danger for everybody. That sort of thing.

Some of it got through. Maybe. The smile dropped, but I was still pretty sure she was not concerned for herself. This can be dangerous. In an operation like this, self-preservation is assumed to be a dependable motivator. Altruists can be unpredictable. Especially when they know only a fraction of what's going on.

"Do exactly what I tell you," I repeated.

"Anything you say." She gave me a mock salute. "Whatever it takes to get the job done. But I hope Keegan won't get hurt. Have you met him? He's half a head shorter than me, but believe me, he makes up for it."

When Diane had gone and I found myself alone in the SCIF, I called my boss over the secure line. It was still morning in England and five hours earlier on the East Coast, but I caught him at home having his first cuppa. Now that he was the boss, his house was equipped with all the gadgets a spook could want, including a secure phone. Frank is a pudgy, bald, nervous man, differing from Nigel in both competence and physical presence. Neither man looks like he can hold his own in a fight, but I happen to know that Frank can do so with deceptive alacrity.

"What's going on?" he said. "The cousins don't seem to like you."

"Good morning to you, too, boss-man," I wondered which cousin he could be hearing from. "The cousins don't like me because of my genetic handicap. I'm female."

"They're saying you're not a good fit for this op."

I had an inkling 'they' consisted of just one man.

"That would be my cousinly colleague. He disappeared for ten hours last night, so we've not been acquainted long enough for him to know. As it turns out, I am a perfect fit."

I thought about that second kiss.

"So, Chicago," I continued.

"What about Chicago? Everything relevant about that op is in the file. Did you read the file?"

He knew I read the file. It was one of the many ways I annoyed the guys in The Section. I always read the files.

"Not CETUS WEDGE," I said. "Earlier."

After an unnaturally long pause, he said, "So what? Sobieski's dead."

Ahhh. He knows about the dangle.

"His, uh, legacy is not."

I packed a great many things into the last comment. I was telling him there was a problem in the current op, that it involved the team dynamics, that a woman was in the mix, that I knew he kept her out of the earlier file to ensure her safety, that the disaster of CETUS WEDGE was not over because the danger to the team's significant others was still extant.

It took him a while to unpack it all.

"Duly noted," he said. "What else?"

He wanted off this topic, so I outlined SIEGE and the bleak future of Lieutenant Colonel Diane Rutherford.

"I think survival here is more important than success," I said. I did not limit this to Diane's survival, because I was beginning to think her continued existence was the key to the survival of the entire team. Catching one IRA assassin whose targets were as yet hypothetical seemed remote in importance compared to the present reality of Diane Rutherford of the twinkly eyes and the effect her demise would have on a set of ruthless killers who had been in the game too long and had seen too much unnecessary carnage.

Did he get all that, I wondered as Frank took the longest pause yet.

"Agreed," he said finally. "You are the best fit for this job. Check in when you can."

…

The cousins were not going to be happy about the realignment of my priorities.

ELEVEN

One of the perks of my job is the chance to see new things. The old things, like jet lag, no sleep, lousy food, and homicidal associates can wear you down after a while, which is why I accepted Diane's invitation to tour the flight-line at RAF Alconbury. Maybe it was a little too public an excursion, but I needed a break. Like the break the toad Nigel took the night before, doing what, I didn't know.

Speaking of toads, we drove past a series of wide concrete bunkers squatting like warty amphibians around a cement pond. Some had their huge doors open, with equipment, generators, and metro vans dotted in among scores of maintenance people dressed in battle dress camouflage uniforms like their commander, my host. I noticed they did not salute her when she stopped to ask a question.

"It's not safe to salute on the flightline," she said when I asked. "Imagine a guy with a wrench in his hand. Does he bean himself or drop it in the airplane? So, this is a no-salute zone. Also, no hats. They can fly off your head straight into an engine."

There were no salutes then, but there were plenty of 'yes ma'ams'—something I had read about in books but never experienced myself. I also belonged to a hierarchical organization, with respectably high rank, above middle management anyway, yet no one ever said yes ma'am to me even figuratively. I get it that in my business the need for creative thinking takes precedence over instant blind obedience, and as a result, we do not encourage outward acknowledgments of rank, but inwardly the hierarchy colors everything, as it does in most organizations.

What I saw on the flightline was more than yes ma'am being said in blind obedience. It was a genuine and general acknowledgment of Diane's authority. I have worked very hard to be as good as or better than every man I have seen in this job. When I make a mistake, though, often the difference between me and the man next to me is that my mistake becomes a monument to the proposition that a woman just cannot hack it in this field.

Diane was clearly hacking it in her field. I resolved in that moment to keep her alive.

We stopped in front of a U-2, called a TR-1 in this part of the world. It reminded me of a video game featuring birds with impossibly long wings flopping up and down. One of these black birds squatted at rest, covered in matte black paint with non-reflective markings, where there were any markings at all. Long red flags attached at various places flapped in the cold English wind. The wings were impossible. They were supported solely by what were called pogos, a single wheel at the end of each wing, designed to fall off once the Dragon Lady became airborne.

Diane's people stayed busy coming and going. Cables and lines of all sorts crisscrossed the tarmac and generators blared. I was impressed.

A metro van pulled up and a spaceman stepped out. Or so it seemed. He was huge and wearing a mustard-colored suit with a space helmet, boots, and gauntlets set into the suit. Tubes snaked from the airplane to ground equipment close by. From the pilot's suit, more tubes were attached to a suitcase he carried with him as he walked a few feet to the airplane. I wondered how they would get this mountain of a man into that small cockpit. It took three people to do it, but they managed without a shoehorn.

We were standing on each side of the truck with the doors open, and I was so fascinated by the scene that I did not notice Diane's silence until a pause in the booming radio chatter gave me a chance to look at her. She stood very still. I was tempted to wave a hand in front of her eyes.

She broke her focus on the cockpit and began to turn away when a radio squawk from the truck announced a problem. Diane walked over to a crew chief wearing a head-set plugged into the front of the aircraft. She took the head-set from him and had a conversation, presumably, with the spaceman in the cockpit. I watched her face. She was all business; no sign of anything else. The only reason it was remarkable is because of the change from the strange pensive quiet of a few moments before.

Other people, these in civilian clothes, began to swarm, each taking a turn on the same headset. Among them, I recognized my agency's Resident. We did not acknowledge each other.

Once the problem was resolved, the Resident came back to the truck with Diane. They were discussing inertial navigation. The subject not being one of my strong suits, in fact not in my wardrobe at all, I did not join them in the conversation. Also, I figured for the sake of security, the Res and I should not be publicly connected. I'd gone to a lot of trouble keeping his identity from Nigel's hounds.

He smiled at Diane and patted her shoulder before leaving. Then he handed me a piece of paper.

So much for my most laudable security consciousness.

I read the paper in the truck while the airplane taxied by in front of us. Diane was discreet, saying nothing about the odd connection between me and the Resident. I'm not sure I could have answered her anyway.

The single page was a telex from Frank, marked SENSITIVE COMPARTMENTED INFORMATION and stamped FLASH. FLASH. FLASH. BARB, COST IS NOT AN ISSUE IN THE SUCCESS OF SIEGE. FRANK."

I felt the ground shake as the airplane left the runway, but I did not hear it roar, because I had my own roaring going on. Someone had called Frank. I already knew that.

Someone told him I was not supporting the operation. I knew who that was now, too.

Now I knew what Nigel had been doing all night. The bastard got hold of my boss. The bastard went behind my back. The bastard.

And, I suspected, he hadn't told Frank the full cost of the American share of SIEGE as I had done just an hour before. I looked at the date time group of the message. Without knowing it, I achieved a reversal of Nigel's dirty work. The sticky part was that his success was in writing. Mine was not.

...

I fumed for an hour while I checked my back, taking the long way home to the safehouse. I drove through The Fens, past huge fields of drained former swampland. It was lovely and flat, mostly cropland with few trees and, it seemed, the only straight roads in Britain. I could see for miles as I checked for tails, but I took no chances. Besides, it allowed me to rehearse what I was going to say to Nigel.

I found him alone in the kitchen, scarfing large portions of the leftover ham.

"You son of a bitch," I said. "What the hell do you think you're doing going to my boss behind my back?"

He spluttered a few upper-class noises, then managed a word or two along the lines of, "Who me?"

"You know very well what you did," I said. "You called my boss."

"No, no I didn't," he insisted. Perhaps the sudden fear in his eyes had something to do with the carving knife I had picked up from the sink. "I only talked to him briefly about that idea I had. Really. That's all."

"Yeah, right. What idea?"

I could see he didn't want to tell me. I carved myself a slice from the ham in front of him. I couldn't help it if the blade just happened to be pointing at his black heart.

"What idea?" I said again.

"Just a small suggestion, the one I told you about early this morning," he said. Nervousness painted his face bright red, and his eyes refused to make contact with mine. They were busy watching the blade.

"Enlighten me again." I vaguely remembered him spouting some ridiculous scheme when all I wanted was sleep.

"What if we had that detonator, *lurve*? What if we could take out anybody we want with a hundred percent reliability? We wouldn't need specialists."

I had to agree I was in a dirty business. He saw my brain work. I can't play poker worth a shit. He began a long string of what-ifs. I managed to insert a question here and there.

"Collateral damage," I said.

He shrugged. "You're always going to have collateral damage."

All well and good unless you are the collaterally damaged.

"Verification."

"We'll verify. Of course, we'll verify, *lurve*."

Of course, you will. Personal vendettas or just plain incompetence never happen in a bureaucracy.

"I'm not your love!" I waved the knife at him.

Allies be damned.

He put up his hands in defense and lost some color, but then sputtered an outline of his plan for accomplishing this utopia. As I listened, I knew I'd never be any kind of love or even like to him. Maybe simmering hate, but that would be best-case.

The man was nuts.

"Anyway," he said, "your boss wants you to cooperate with me on this."

"Did he say that?"

Nigel didn't have much of a poker face, either. More of a sunburned blowfish face.

"He said something to you," he said, "or you wouldn't have come in here swearing at me like a fishwife."

I reflected a moment, hating Nigel in his brief minor triumph. I went over every word of Frank's message. It had burned itself into my memory.

"Did you tell him about Rutherford?" I asked.

"Well, no, I did not. I just told him about your whining in general."

That searing internal blast of aha! along with an accompanying boatload of anger clarified the rest of the message for me. Frank had given me an order concerning the more ordinary costs of SIEGE, a properly verified, diplomatically cleared operation put together by our allies. He was specifically telling me not to join in Nigel's goofy ad hoc bid for glory. And I now had it verbally straight from Frank that Rutherford was my priority.

"Who picked Rutherford?" I asked.

I could see wheels turning behind Nigel's eyes.

"I don't recall," he lied.

So Nigel picked her. "Why?"

There were sputters and eye rolls before he managed "Um. She. Um. I didn't know she was a woman! The list of names just gave initials. She's an electrical engineer, a military commander, for God's sake, how was I to know? Tell me that. She's got the chops to be believable and she's agreeable. She's perfect for God's sake!"

Agreeable like the dangle in Chicago had been agreeable. Instinct told me somehow this little piece of incompetence was part of the puzzle. Instinct, and the rising hysteria in Nigel's voice. He knew it, too.

I smiled. When I raised the knife for another slice of ham, Nigel watched the blade and blanched completely, red face to white, just as the team walked through the kitchen door to see it. Sweet.

I had a fraction of a second to enjoy the spectacle of him running away from me and out the door, spouting nonsense about things to do.

Mack rummaged in the refrigerator while Charlie and Louis arranged themselves at the big farm table. Steve grabbed the last of the ham and headed back to the drawing room to watch the sensors.

I stood by the sink, savoring my momentary illusion of power. Mack closed the refrigerator door, demanded lunch, and even snapped his fingers at me.

I had just vanquished one son of a bitch. I was ready to take on the next.

"What?" I said. "Your arm broken?"

"You say you are competent," he said. "Get me some competent lunch, woman."

He spat the last word. I was already on top of old Smokey, and it was about to blow.

"Get it yourself, maaaan." I stretched out that last word, giving it all the contempt I had in me, which was considerable at the moment.

I got the cold blue glare that has made the man famous in certain unsavory circles.

"But I am not an award-winning cook," he said slowly.

"Neither am I."

"But you are."

I did not like his growing confidence on the topic of me, a subject I hold dear and very, very private, especially in, again, certain unsavory circles. Even more, I became more than uneasy as he became very still.

"You won first place for your pickles when you were, let me see," he lifted his chin a fraction as if to calculate something, "just thirteen years old."

It had been a point of pride back then at the Nebraska State Fair. Now, and here, not so much. But I never turn down an invitation to spar.

"So what do you want pickled for lunch?" I asked. "Your balls?"

He smiled ever so slowly. Never a good sign.

"Why don't you wear the pink chiffon dress you wore to the prom when you were sixteen?" he said. "Will it not fit? Did your date like it, the one who stood no higher than your shoulder? Did he offer to take it off of you? Did he force it off of you? Did he succeed?"

I caught his sideways glance at Louis.

"And tell us about the baby you had at seventeen," he continued. "Was your prom date the father? Why did the baby die? Did he kill your baby? Is that why you prefer the company of violent men? Are we sufficiently violent for your tastes? So no husband, no baby, no kitchen drudgery, no warm body on a cold night, and no strings to tie you down. Empty. No longer so awkward, but still so empty, and always at risk by your own poor choices."

Geez, these guys knew how to gather intel.

I stalked out the door and stood shaking in the hallway. Crying was not an option, but I was so very tired. An arm came around my shoulders and I looked up at Louis. He was rested for a change. The circles under his eyes had lightened, but were the eyes full of concern, or was I just imagining it?

He led me upstairs to the room he used. I protested. He made me lie down, covered me with a blanket, and said, "I will wake you in three hours."

He was babysitting his babysitter.

He stopped at the door. "You should not enter the cage like a matador, *mon cher*. You must tame Misha not goad him, because you will have no chance against him that way. He will know how best to hurt you."

TWELVE

I fell asleep in an instant and awoke again an instant later. Steve was on top of me, busy with the button on my jeans and relishing the fight I was putting up.

"Fuck, Steve," I said.

"That's the general idea." He nuzzled my neck.

"Get off me, you son of a bitch," I fought furiously against a multi-level black belt martial artist and tried not to think about the odds.

"It's my turn," he said as he covered my mouth with his. My sports bra slipped upward, with my struggle only aiding the effort.

I felt a weight shifting on the bed.

"A little fucking privacy would be nice," said Steve, breaking the kiss. As my t-shirt finished coming off over my head, I looked up into a pair of hard blue eyes and knew I was sunk.

"There is no privacy on this team," said Charlie. He was sitting with his back against the headboard and legs stretched out alongside our battleground.

I continued to fight, found an opening, and bit Steve's arm.

"Ow! Fuck," said Steve. "Don't distract me, Charlie."

"This is not a good idea."

I agreed with Charlie.

"You want a threesome?" said Steve.

For the first time in this op, I wasn't just afraid. I was terrified.

"No, I want her gone. We will all be dead by tomorrow if we cannot behave as a team."

"So let's team up with a threesome."

"My purpose was to convince her to leave," said Charlie. "To show her she has no chance against us. What is your purpose?"

His immediate purpose was to remove my jeans. They were coming down steadily.

"Pure payback," said Steve.

I was in the fight of my life and had no contribution to make to the conversation besides a frenzied effort to keep my pants on. He pinned one hand above my head.

"For what?" said Charlie.

"The nickname, for one thing."

"It would not have stuck if it were not apt. You do look like a teddy bear."

Steve paused to glare at him.

"Okay. You are not a teddy bear. You only look like one," said Charlie, hands raised. "What other reason?"

"She belongs to The Section. They all want to do this, so this is for them. They made my life hell after CETUS WEDGE, so this is to them. Pick one."

"Fuck, Steve. What have you and I been doing the last few days? Certainly not concentrating on coming out of the operation alive. How will my father ever trust you after this?"

There was a pause, then a nip at my neck, next to the one from Charlie, then a sigh, and finally, "Shit." Steve removed his fingers, let go of my hand, and rolled off me. He headed for the door.

Charlie looked down at me with a raised eyebrow and smug expression before following Steve.

I contemplated a career change while putting my clothes back on, sobbing quietly and thinking about flight schedules out of Heathrow. This was the lowest I had ever been, even counting all that had happened in Nebraska, every crazy group of villains I had dealt with on the job, all the dirt and the violence and the pain. This was the worst. I hadn't been fully penetrated, but near enough and now put in mortal dread of it. And I knew it was still not the best way to hurt me, as Louis would say. I was ready to pack and get out before that happened.

Then a spark of anger lit a slow burn in me. I had struggled and fought for so long to do this impossible job and was about to be robbed of it by two testosterone-crazed delinquents with hot and cold reasons for wanting to make me sorry to be a woman. I am not sorry. I'm glad of it and unashamed of what I consider to be my strength, not my weakness.

I decided I preferred Steve's hot reasoning. I was indeed a pain in the ass in The Section, but they would nonetheless consider me one of theirs if something happened to me. And they did bully Steve without mercy. It was all within the bounds of human behavior, and I could deal with it.

Charlie's cold calculation was not. There was no room for mercy in it. Circumstances might limit him, but compassion did not. He was indeed more dangerous than his father.

As I curled tightly into a ball, with unending silent tears descending to the pillow, I remembered Diane Rutherford. I was the only person, besides Louis perhaps,—and only perhaps—who wanted her to live. My resolve to stay and struggle solidified even as I allowed myself the luxury of falling asleep while a complete basket case.

I woke when I felt the all too familiar weight of someone sitting on the mattress. I had learned fight was impossible, uncurled myself, and launched into flight. A hand held my t-shirt, stopping me before I could get a foot on the floor. Louis took both my shoulders and turned me to face him. He sat exactly as Charlie had done but with longer legs and held me firmly while he examined my face. I knew my eyes would be puffy and my reaction would be telling. I also could not hide the trepidation in my mind that I was in for another session of intimidation and payback, this time with the most formidable foe of all, precisely because I did not want him as an enemy.

He sighed. "Did Steve succeed?"

Of course he knew, I realized. They all instinctively knew where everybody else was. It meant Mack knew, as well.

"Only as far as Charlie did," I said as if the word 'only' had any use at all in this context.

"Was there a reason?"

"Payback."

He nodded. "A grudge, then. That was also my reason."

"They had an entire fucking conversation while… while…" I felt the tears burning my sore eyes again.

He took a clean handkerchief from his pocket and dabbed my face with it. We were surrounded by filth and squalor and he smelled like the unwashed, unshaven, broken-nosed killer he was, but he had a clean handkerchief in his pocket. Go figure. At least he had it until it came in contact with the mascara streaming down my face. He then required me to recount the entire fucking conversation, in those words, as closely as possible to the original.

"Charlie is right," he said. "You should leave."

I did not mention Diane, the survival of the team—of far lesser importance to me right then—or the survival of my career. "I won't let them destroy me," I said.

He gave me an inimical look and said coolly, "I am one of them. If you stay you likely will be destroyed."

"If I go, I most certainly will be."

"You did not fight my kiss as you did those two. Why?"

How to explain desire? I considered the question before answering, "Your kiss was an offer. Theirs was a taking."

"Sometimes," he said, "a man must risk being mistaken in order to create the offer."

"Oh, we often want men to try. We always want the right to decline."

"I guarantee you will not decline the next time I try." He smacked my thigh, swung his feet to the floor, and said, "Go. Make yourself presentable before you come downstairs. Misha will know what happened anyway, but you should try some concealment if only to save Steve a serious tongue-lashing."

Tongue lashing? If I had my way, he'd be beaten to a pulp.

THIRTEEN

L ooking refreshed and presentable, but not feeling it, I entered the drawing room feeling rather chuffed that I was still alive. Everybody was there. Louis sat back in one of the wingback chairs facing the sole source of heat, the fireplace burning a small heap of coal. He was reading the latest transcripts of various taps on everybody's private lives.

Charlie sat in another chair farther back from the fire, glued to the sensor console. It occurred to me that cold was his natural element. I had an uncle who would have said, "That boy ain't right." It was not a comforting thought. Steve lay sprawled along the three-legged sofa, drifting in and out of sleep.

Mack occupied the other wingback chair by the fire, cleaning his weapon. Despite their current difficulties with each other, the group acknowledged Mack and Louis as the senior decision-makers and treated them accordingly. When they weren't busy throwing them against walls to prevent murder, that is.

Nigel was making a new pot of coffee. This explained why everybody ignored me. I was comfortable with that, but

I forced myself into a renewed dedication to the job at hand and decided it was time to call a meeting.

I stood before the fire, enjoying the warmth on my backside, and screwed up my courage to address the room. After a few polite starts that went nowhere and interested no one because evidently, I was invisible, I brought out my command voice.

"Listen up! We are going to discuss this op using The Method to see whether we can determine the most helpful hypotheses to use in going forward."

Too many big words. I tried again.

"I'm talking about the various steps we should run the information through, like examining assumptions, quality of information, potential for change, and so on."

"That's analysis," said Nigel. "It's what the women do. We're operatives. We don't have time for that shit."

Charlie raised an eyebrow at his use of the word 'we' and turned up one corner of his lips in a half smile that made me concerned for Nigel's safety. Almost concerned, I should say. I would be fully concerned if I cared more.

Mack looked up from his gun and contemplated my face. It is the best word to describe that searching stare. I had used eyedrops, powder, eye shadow, and mascara creatively, but his blue eyes were too intent. I began to stutter.

"If… f… f w… we can get a firm grasp on what we know about Cú Chulainn we may be able to identify him and take him out before he meets Rutherford. We should start by examining our assumptions. What's the most rock-solid thing we think we know about Cú Chulainn?"

Steve, bless his black heart, broke the ice for me. "His tradecraft is perfect."

Mack tore his searching gaze from his son's studied impassivity and transferred it to Steve, who knew it and whose face immediately told Mack everything he wanted to know.

"Evidence?" I asked.

"We don't know who the fuck he is." Steve had decided to brave it out.

There was a quiet chuckle all around, except Mack, whose eyes were on Louis.

"What else?" I continued.

"He's Irish," said Nigel with a smirk.

"Again, what's our evidence for that?" I felt the cold blue gaze back on me.

"He blows up Englishmen," said Steve.

Nigel bit his lip before saying, "Teague, the cutout, is unquestionably Irish."

"But couldn't Cú Chulainn be a solo specialist working for the IRA?" I said. "Couldn't they just hire him from time to time? It might explain the impossibly deep cover."

"The IRA is not sufficiently funded to hire a specialist of this class," said Louis. "He is in house."

"It is always about money with you!" exploded Mack. He threw down the patch he had been threading onto a cleaning rod. His gun was in pieces; *thank heaven for small mercies*, but the knife was still somewhere on him.

Steve moved in front of Louis and Charlie in front of Mack before the next breath and I was smack dab in the middle. I heard expletives in three languages used with imagination and ingenuity.

"You put your filthy hands on her to betray me, you son of a bitch!"

"You were fucking indecent, the both of you, every morning at breakfast, she with her blushes and you smiling, damn you, smiling! All the time smiling!"

Evidently, smiling was something not generally done at the breakfast table at Vasily's Carpet. I could relate. I grew up on a farm. There was a lot more back and forth about how disgusting they both were. Again, I could relate, until Louis pointed to me.

"She agrees with me," said Louis. "This had nothing to do with you."

That's not exactly what I said, but explanations were superfluous under that blue gaze. "What does it have to do with, Miss Kemp?" Mack asked softly, politely, with his hands in fists and a vein standing out along the side of his scarred neck. "Is it your theory," he spat the word, "that my wife was asking for it? Did she wear her dress too short? Was there too much makeup? Did she provoke his lust?"

"Of course not," I said with some vehemence. I noticed Charlie give Steve a signal with the smallest eye movement and Steve hustled Louis out of the room to do a perimeter check. I was left under the incredibly still stare of four blue eyes, with Nigel the only other person in the room. He was busily making himself as invisible as possible by trying not to breathe.

"You will tell me," said Mack, "what you think this is about."

I had no idea what it was about. I had gone through the looking glass so many times all I had in my brain was the phrase, *off with her head*. So I was left with pulling something out of my ass. Now, it seems perfect and profound. At the time, it was a pathetic evasion that was likely to get me killed in the next instant.

"Listen to his words and his voice," I said. "They tell you why it happened."

He gave a disgusted snort, picked up the pieces of his gun, and told Nigel to meet him in the dining room with the layout of the place we thought would be the venue of Cú Chulainn's demise.

I was left alone with just the young pair of blue eyes vacuuming my mind until it became a void.

"No fists thrown," I said, trying to smile. "Nothing un- sheathed or unholstered. That's progress, don't you think?"

Charlie's stillness as he regarded me was freakier than his father's had been. "You are a disruption," he said finally. "If I were in charge, you would be dead now."

There is no snappy comeback for this, nor any assertive rejoinder, nor suitable question even. Groveling for mercy was beneath my dignity; even if I thought it might help, I would not demean myself. I clamped down on my expression like a drill sergeant with a platoon of conscripts, willing myself to show no concern. I tried a slight glare of defiance but could not help the hard swallow my throat demanded from me.

He was satisfied with that, the bastard, and walked away.

FOURTEEN

Keegan was a very dull boy. He hadn't called Diane or come over for two days. We knew he was in town because of the very light touch Nigel had on his car. This put us in boredom mode for a couple of hours that late afternoon and we used it according to our various talents. I organized the refrigerator. Louis taught Steve how to program the device. Mack didn't kill Louis. I didn't kill Nigel. Charlie didn't kill me. All in all, things were working out.

I took a few quiet moments to contemplate Nigel's plan for getting his grubby little hands on the detonator. I came up with questions I should have asked him at the time. Could that even be done, stealing from his own team, without getting himself killed? He said he had another team ready to help him, led by some guy named Stan. Did he intend to set up a different specialist team to attack his own? It made no sense. But so far on this op, that was nothing new. There were too many treacherous intentions mixing with sharp objects for my comfort.

Louis read more transcripts from Life of Diane and grilled me about her charms. I reminded myself this was business; the man meant a promotion for me, nothing more.

"What is this word you use, twinkly?" he said. "What does it mean?"

"Twinkly. Her eyes are twinkly. They twinkle."

"Then why do you not say that? Why not say only 'her eyes twinkle' instead of 'her eyes are twinkly.'"

"Because it is more than an occasional verb," I said. "It is a quality of the eyes that is always there. The eyes don't *do* a twinkle; they *are* twinkly."

"And you are strange."

Evidently, strange was on the menu today. Louis was so delighted not to be dead (yet) he invited me to celebrate with him. Upstairs. Where he had some etchings to show me.

I declined with a sigh several times that afternoon, each episode accompanied by heavy breathing. On my part.

"Forget it," I said finally. "You need a bath."

"We can bathe together." His dark eyes twinkled. Verb-wise.

"What about Diane?"

He wrinkled his forehead. "She is words on a page; you are real." His hands were busy kneading my bottom.

"But strange," I said.

He put his arm around my waist. "Oh yes, very strange. Come. I shall die in a few hours. My last wish is yours to grant."

How many times have I heard that line?

The tub was in the bedroom he had been using. It stood on claw feet by the boarded-up window, was long and deep, and had two faucets specializing in freezing and scalding water. We soaped and scrubbed and had a water fight. There were no towels, but it didn't matter. We dried off naturally on the bed, staying warm by making love like we had been together forever. It was so joyous an act, I had no time to regret the reality around us.

He asked obliquely if I had ever done this before, as he kissed my neck. I was confused at first. I've never been mistaken for a virgin, even when I was one. But he wanted to know if I'd ever had sex with my team members before. I didn't answer right away because by this time he was sucking one nipple and playing with the other and my mind was elsewhere. No, I gasped. Why? He reached my navel, with both hands on my breasts, every caress making me ache for him. *What is this, an essay exam?* I don't find specialists all that attractive as a rule, I told him. I felt each touch of his tongue on all the nerves of my body simultaneously, a deliciously warm electrical charge buzzing everywhere, but especially between my legs. But you find me attractive, he wanted to know as he reached the zone of awesomeness.

I find you incredible.

I might have screamed that last bit.

After a lot more incredible awesomeness, in several positions and all with vigor, we flopped, side by side. I glowed. He snored.

"I told Mack you never meant to steal his wife," I said during a break in the snoring.

"You did what?"

"I told him this morning before I left to meet Diane."

Louis chuckled and looked at me. "No wonder he is so fond of you. Misha would consider the topic to be not your business. What did he say?"

Louis was eager and curious, like a child. I suspected, no I knew, I was in this too deep. But I could not explain, even to myself, what was wrong here, and I had begun to think our collective survival depended on knowing what it was.

"He said something like it might be true in one sense but not every sense and anyway I was as stupid as you, but he shouldn't expect anything more from a spinster like me."

Louis' brow wrinkled. "What did that mean?"

I shrugged. "I asked him that."

Louis patted my thigh. "You are so brave," he said. "Sometimes I think you are not very bright."

"I think the world of you, too, Stud Muffin."

We then discussed a string of American idioms, each one prompted by an explanation of the one before it. After I inadvertently expanded the never-ending list by telling him I was no fuddy-duddy, I steered us back on course. "Do you want to know what he said?"

He nodded.

"He said when you hurt her, you hurt him. Thus, you betrayed him."

"He has said that before," said Louis. "It is not true. He is not her. She is not him. And I did not hurt her. I raped her."

"I did tell him it seemed he was more concerned about some boundary around his property than he was with compassion for her."

And I'm not convinced you raped her, I thought, but I kept my own counsel on that.

"I do not understand," he said.

I spoke carefully. "I think men can behave as if harm to someone they love, especially a woman, is an affront to their manhood rather than a crime against the woman."

"But everyone is upset when a loved one is harmed. It is a good way to intimidate a man. Threaten his women."

"Yes, but especially in cases of the rape of a woman, its aftermath can be more about the man than the traumatized person herself. This is the impression I have from the entire team. Even you."

He looked at me with question marks above his eyebrows.

"I can't believe you would ever rape a woman. Seduce, yes. Rape, no." I said, not sure if I could ever get him to understand or even if I fully understood. It made me nervous not knowing the limits of this conversation.

"We are all capable of all things, good and bad," he said. "Rape is rage. It is always rage, against one person, against all people, against powerlessness."

"Powerless against what?"

He was silent.

"You could have just beaten her," I said, "or shot her. Why rape?"

He did not answer for a moment, and I expected a repeat of the 'best way to hurt her' stuff. I was wrong.

He said, "She does not like me."

There are so many reasons, so many aggravating factors, so many mitigating factors, that classifying any given rape is stupid.

"It always boils down to an act of violence," I said. Aloud this time. "Even when the victim submits to it."

"I am a violent man," he said. "Why is everybody so surprised?"

"But rape? It deranges the very core of a person's identity. Other assaults are exterior; rape is interior. It is monstrous and you are not a monster."

He turned his head to look at me. Black hair against a white pillow. His eyes, also nearly black, regarded me.

"I kill to live," he said. "Of course, I am a monster. Again I ask, why are you surprised?" He got up and started looking for his clothes. "And besides, Alex should not have told Misha about it. I blame her for all the trouble."

You are a unique form of bastard, sweetie, and…. I lost that particular train of thought when her name hit whatever brain center filing cabinet it is that stores such things in an intelligence agent. I had known it all along, of course, if I had been paying attention, but the spoken name made the connection real and present.

"Alex?" I might have screeched it. "Not Sobieski's widow?" I had thought it was the history, from one doomed dangle to the latest one with the twinkly eyes, that complicated the current madness. This threw a lot more puzzle pieces into place. My intuition had been spot on.

He nodded. "It was a surprise to everybody. They married last autumn. Vasily and Katya were not yet cold in their graves."

I wondered why a killer who faces sudden death himself at almost every moment could be so bitter about these two deaths. Or were the dead making themselves silently convenient for hiding the living people who bugged him?

"I thought Alex and Misha did not get along," I said.

"They didn't. They don't. They argue. But they are best friends as well as lovers. They are disgusting."

"Louis," I said, "you know she didn't have to tell him. He reads minds."

He looked at me for a long moment.

"He was not reading your mind in the kitchen today, Barbara. I found that information about you. We gather as much as we can on everyone in your section. Did you think you were the only ones who created files?"

"But the dress?"

"A picture in your high school yearbook."

I digested this slowly, suddenly conscious of the stretch marks on my belly, the bullied scars on my psyche. Had he seen them? Should I tell him that the farm girl in that picture and I were not the same person anymore? I waited until I had control of a threatening teardrop before turning my head to look at him.

He gazed at me without judgment.

"But you are correct," he said. "Alex did not have to tell him."

FIFTEEN

I made sure the long upstairs hallway was empty before scooting out and across to the room where I had stowed my suitcase. I was in no condition to exchange how d'ya do's with anybody who might nod in a friendly way to a tall woman topped by a nest of dark hair hanging in snarls and with a rather satisfied look on her face. I carried my clothes and did not bother to close the bathrobe Louis had loaned me for the twenty-foot scurry.

I was within five feet of my destination when a door opened to my left. I jumped like a six-foot bunny. It was Mack. When I saw his face, I prepared to run. Prepared as in releasing all the adrenaline necessary for the flight portion of the human response to an emergency. The fight portion was out of the question. For one thing, I was pretty much naked. Funny how being naked makes you feel especially vulnerable—as if a few yards of cotton or wool or rayon or viscose are the ultimate talisman against a bullet or Mack's knife.

Flight was also not an option. Before my brain could motivate my feet, I was against the wall, pinned by Mack's hand around my throat.

He was furious. Not with jealousy, of course. I can feel a man's interest as palpably as a soft blanket on a thorn bush. Mack genuinely couldn't stand the sight of me. He said some things I could not answer because it takes breath to operate the vocal cords and my breath was absent for the moment. His questions all boiled down to a confused "Why?"

He loosened his grip just enough for me to croak an answer.

"He needed comfort," I said.

We both became aware at the same instant that Charlie had come up the stairs and stood to my left, Mack's right, staring.

"What are you looking at?" said Mack.

"A scene I remember in Vasily's Carpet," said Charlie, "the morning after we came back from Chicago last year. But it was Louis who had Alex by the throat. He said what you said. And when he let her speak, that was how she answered."

Mack glared at him but let me go suddenly and pushed past his son, leaving us to stare at each other in the empty hall.

Charlie's face was expressionless.

I already knew his opinion and let go of another involuntary hard swallow. It registered with him and he let me squeeze past him.

...

"This is not a good idea," I insisted. "If we meet Diane in public and Cú Chulainn gets wind of us, he will fly!"

Steve put on his patient look. "Let me explain this again, Barb. We don't know how soon Teague will ask for the demo. If he wants it tomorrow morning, we're sunk unless we do this tonight. I have to brief the colonel. So I must be introduced."

"I've described you to her," I said. I picked up my comb again. My hair was still a giant tangle. We sat on a sofa in the drawing room. Charlie sat across from us in a decrepit leather wingback chair that leaned on a crooked leg. Despite the squalor around him, he looked like he belonged to the world of leather chairs and fine cigars. Louis fiddled with his gadgets in the transcript room across the hall. Nigel and Mack were doing the perimeter rounds, checking the sensors.

It had begun as a peaceful evening. I should have had plenty of time to untangle my hair, but Nigel's people picked up a phone call and rushed the transcript to us. Keegan had asked Diane out to dinner.

"Will your description of me suffice when I approach her at two in the morning?" said Steve.

"Okay, but I still don't see why I have to go," I said. "I could blow the whole thing. It's dangerous." I winced as I pulled at a knot. As that resolved under my comb, the one in my stomach grew. I did not want to get in a car with Steve.

He and Charlie exchanged a private comment by rolling their eyes.

"It's dangerous to the op," I insisted. "I don't mean to me personally!" I could see they did not understand. "Look, Steve, Cú Chulainn himself is going to be there, and if he's as good as you say he is, he'll know I'm not your type. He may even know me from an earlier op. I've been around for a dozen years in this business. It's too risky."

There was a serious silence.

"What makes you think Cú Chulainn will be there?" said Charlie.

"He'll want to check out the colonel himself. If he's that good, I mean. If I were Cú Chulainn, that's what I would do."

They both blew air through their teeth.

"Well, let's thank our luck you are not Cú Chulainn, then," said Charlie.

...

I received no oohs or ahs as I came downstairs to the men waiting in the hall. Nobody said a word about my flawless jade-green dress or the way my thick chocolate hair swung freely about my waist. Instead, I heard, "Come on, damn it," and, "Where the hell is she?"

They stood at the foot of the stairs fidgeting with their ties or staring at the front door, hands in pockets. Louis had shaved. He wore a clean suit and looked like the man of my dreams, tall, handsome and tall. He smiled at me. Mack glared at me, evidently relishing his role as the man of my nightmares. Everybody, even Nigel, bless him, looked presentable, though only Steve and I would be seen in public.

As we filed out the door, Nigel mumbled into my ear, "New competitive edge, is it? Offering them, or at least the Frenchman, something other babysitters can't?"

I looked him in his bloodshot eyes. "Why? Were you wishing you could offer the same?"

It was an offhand remark, meant as an insult, as it would be to many of the men in my business, but Nigel's reaction surprised me. I hoped I had hidden my surprise better than he masked his blush. Well, well, well, my dear enemy, I thought. Now I have you by the balls. One word, one hint from me, and fifteen years of service are over in the space of a sigh. They won't be likely to go near you, except maybe to cut your throat.

I found myself reluctantly admiring my rival. To spend fifteen years near these guys, especially Mack the mind reader, while giving no hint of his secret took considerable professional skill. I suddenly had newfound respect for Nigel but stashed my ultimate weapon in a safe but accessible place in my memory, in case I might someday need to use it.

If our new shared understanding altered my attitude toward Nigel, it seemed like it did the same for his attitude toward me, or at least his behavior. He respectfully opened the car door for me. Steve and I were taking Nigel's Jaguar.

The others would follow, Mack and Charlie in the Mercedes, Louis and Nigel in the heap.

As he started the car, Steve began our evening together with a lecture. He is one of those drivers who cannot maintain a steady acceleration. Or maybe his topic made him start and stop without reason until I was glad my stomach was empty because it was threatening to spew like a volcano. Unlike his driving, Steve's words came smoothly, punctuated by rhetorical question marks. Did I know how disgusting it was to see me and Louis smiling at each other? Like a couple of teenagers at a school dance? And anyway, didn't I realize the man was made of stone? Or, was I some kind of masochist? Huh? Did I know he's a rapist? Or doesn't that cut any wood with a feminist unless the victim is also a feminist? Wives and mothers don't count?

"That's rich coming from you," I said. "As I recall, none of that mattered to you a few hours ago. Also, he's paying for it, more than he would in a court of law and maybe soon he'll pay a lot more than that." I did not mention my reservations about the truth of the accusation. Even Louis was still maintaining his guilt, though I had challenged him on it several times. I think it was the hesitation in his answers, among other things, that made me continue to question it.

"Not enough," said Steve. "He's not paying enough. You haven't met her. It's like destroying innocence itself, which does not apply to you. And none of us, least of all Misha, appreciates you giving Louis a conjugal visit."

"That's especially rich coming from all you guys, Steve, considering that for all practical purposes, Mack raped her in the first place."

He slammed on the brakes and skidded to a stop on the side of the road.

"What the fuck are you talking about? What rape? She was Sobieski's wife in the first place. In the second place, you don't know shit about them."

"I know more than you think, Steve. I actually read the files, remember that about me?"

And pillow talk is the richest source of nutrition in espionage, but I left this little bit out. I was already rueing the fact that I brought it up at all. Information like this loses its value when it is spread too thin.

"Tell me," he said when he made the pillow talk connection.

I hesitated. "It's not pillow talk," I said. "He told me during one of our watches together. You can probably get it just by asking."

He grabbed my throat so fast, it took my breath away, and so hard, there was no way to suck in some more. He released a little pressure but kept his hold and said again, "Tell me."

I knew he was capable of violence, but it had now become his go-to reaction in all scenarios. I set aside my impulse to horde the information he wanted and told him, between gasps, about the card game some fourteen years before.

Charlie walked past the headlights to my side of the car. Steve reached to operate the electric window. "What?" he said.

"It looks like there is a problem," said Charlie. "I'll be happy to help you kill her anytime, though I know you're quite capable."

"Yeah, thanks," said Steve. "Not this time."

He let go and I massaged my throat.

I was tempted to bring up my misgivings, about doomed dangles, about questions of consent and rape versus seduction, among other things, but Steve had become an alien creature. As a fellow babysitter he might have been able to view the issue in a practical way, but he was no longer a babysitter, and I had the bruises to prove it. As for making some kind of human connection, that was foreclosed by the subject. He was the most male individual I had ever met and had shown me too much of his intentions towards me. I would get further by explaining Cinderella to a Martian.

...

I had to duck through the low medieval doorway at the Cock and Bull, or whatever the hell they call it, in Godmanchester. The ceiling was not comfortable either, with low-hanging beams that threatened my dignity every time my forehead connected with one. I tried to stay within the troughs between them, but that sometimes made me move sideways like a spider crab. I don't remember a time when I wasn't the tallest girl in the family or the class or the room. I'm used to being conspicuous. Diane and I were bound to be remembered in that room that night, and I worried about it. Cú Chulainn would be there for sure, whether Steve and Charlie thought so or not.

I thought I'd give it one more try to warn Steve. If I failed, hey, I would have done my job. So I tried to catch his eye as we made our way to the bar, but something or someone else was way ahead of me. The alarm on his face said it all. He was in some trouble of his own.

SIXTEEN

"**D**an!"

Steve turned white. I thought he was going to faint. An enormous figure moved across the room toward us, ducking ceiling beams, with a wide grin and outstretched arms.

Steve stood frozen. I prepared to catch him on his way to the floor.

"Whaddayadooinhere?" The sound echoed off the walls and the booming voice continued, "Haven't seen you since pilot training!"

The giant grabbed Steve's hand and threatened to pump his arm off at the shoulder. Then came a back slap and "Whaddayadrinkin?"

Steve fell back on his training and did the only thing he could. He went on the offensive, returning the backslap, getting loud, and sticking to his legend.

"Mace! Great to see you! Small world! I'm over here working for Hughes. What are you doing these days?"

There followed a loud exchange in which one was flying the TR-1, the designation of the U-2 in Europe, and loving it, and the other was Steve's total fiction. I wondered, was he loving it?

This was a surprise, something people in my field do not like, and it was monumental. The situation deepened my already gloomy prognostication about the evening. Mace was a recent boyfriend of Diane's. For some reason, he didn't count as being of interest in Nigel's professional opinion. But the man's presence now, which would have been expected if there had been just the lightest touch on his activity, was threatening the entire op. *Oh, Nigel.*

A woman I had not yet noticed joined Mace, putting an immediate and rather depressing damper on the boisterous reminiscing. Mace began introductions.

"Fiona!"

I don't think Mace could speak without an exclamation point.

"Fiona, look who's here! An old buddy of mine from pilot training...."

"Steve Donovan," Steve interrupted, his voice low and smooth as whipped butter. He took her hand, bowed over it, and kissed the back of it. Hokey, but brilliant.

The maneuver held her attention, giving Mace time to mask his shock. His performance also was flawless. "Steve and I go way back," he said without a hiccup.

Within five minutes I knew Diane was a fool to give this guy up. It wasn't just his enormity, though being tall is always a desirable manly trait in my book. It was his hearty goodwill. His black eyes sparkled with friendship. His wide Polynesian face smiled easily. He had a quick wit and a firm handshake, making you feel like he was on your side. It almost made me forget Louis.

If Diane made a mistake in letting him go, Mace wasn't doing any better in his choice of a replacement. I took an instant dislike to Fiona and found myself judging her mousy brown hair, sensible shoes, and nondescript dress printed with one of those little flower patterns. I suppose she was pretty in a way, but I see no beauty in domestic doormats. Why Mace would trade the stately Diane for this ostensibly fertile stick figure was beyond me. The worst thing about her was she was not stupid, as I would have expected from household breeding stock. I watched her observe the room sharply. I wondered if the homely manner was a put-on designed to capture one large American pilot. She seemed to have succeeded. He was very attentive.

Diane and Keegan showed up and we went through the introductions a second time with everybody acting surprised to see everybody else. I searched the room for Cú Chulainn. Who could it be? The bar was filling quickly. It was hard to tell because just as I had predicted, Diane and I drew more than the usual stares. I figured Cú Chulainn would not openly stare and contemplated the few men who did not seem to notice us, but none of them seemed likely; too old, too young, too out of shape.

We did the ladies-to-the-ladies room routine, all together now, the three of us, leaving the men to discuss airplanes. Or, I should say, leaving Teague to listen while Steve and Mace discussed airplanes. I don't think Steve noticed I had left or even remembered why he was there. He seemed to think he had come to talk about the TR-1 because that was all he did that night.

Diane and I engaged in a sign language and lip-reading conversation while Fiona was in a stall.

"Him?" said Diane silently.

I nodded.

"When?"

"Tonight."

She nodded.

There was still an evening to get through. A night of fun and frolics before Steve and Diane got to work. Diane had fun. I got the frolics.

When Mace headed down the hallway leading to the toilets, I excused myself again, acting a little tipsy to cover the second trip, and waved Diane back into her seat.

It helped that the hallway was narrow. I had no trouble getting close.

"Hi." I gave him my most knowing (and knowable) smile and swung my hair about my shoulders. I looked up at him. Way up. The man made me feel like a pixie sprite.

"Hi."

Evidently a man of few words, he acted like he wanted to get past me. I did not let him.

"You're a friend of Diane's aren't you?" I said, putting my hand on his arm. "She told me about you. We should have coffee sometime. What about tomorrow?"

"Why?"

"Well, I'm new here and need to meet people. You'd be a good start since we have a friend in common."

"What about your friend Steve?" He lifted his chin toward the pub lounge and stressed the name.

"Oh, him? He's a blind date. I'm not sure we're hitting it off." I gave him a smile that I hoped explained what I meant by hitting it off.

Mace looked down on me with a serious scrutiny that made me glad he flew an airplane armed with a camera. He'd be scary with missiles. He considered for a long time before saying, "My guess is you're some kind of spook and this is official, so yeah, I'll meet you tomorrow or any time you like. Coffee's not necessary. But if I'm wrong and you're just some stranger who wants to talk about me and Diane, I'll pass."

"Fair enough." I dropped the smile. "I'll meet you at the SCIF at seven."

"O-seven? Just to be clear," he said.

"Yes. O-seven."

SEVENTEEN

The radio in Nigel's Jaguar stopped working, bringing us down to just two cars. Steve and Louis holed up in the Mercedes to go over the program again, so I was shunted to the heap with the others, parked in a copse near a little village called Abbot's Ripton, a straight radio shot from the base. From the moment they arrived at her apartment at eleven o'clock, we heard every breath Diane and Teague took. They did a lot of breathing.

I was groggy and punch-drunk from fatigue. The few hours of sleep I managed to steal that day were long worn off. I guess that's why I did it. That and the moans and other little noises coming from the radio made me uncomfortable, sitting as I was next to Mack in the back seat behind Nigel and Charlie in front. Maybe it was an unconscious attempt not to listen.

Mack leaned up against the door, huffing or snarling every time I moved, sighing, scowling, and growling at me. I don't like people who do not like me. I don't know why, but it is automatic, and I return that dislike immediately. I suppose it's because I have no patience with people who don't have the good sense to recognize all of my fine qualities. Mack was certainly in that category of person. It was a pity, because he had such a reputation for being a good judge of character, though he was also known to like only very few people.

I knew I was not destined to be one of those people, so I took it as a kind of special license. We sat there in the car with a good two hours of soft-porn listening yet to go, and I felt like I'd been shut into a nail-studded coffin, nails pointing in. When Mack started the snarling nonsense, I decided to give him something to snarl about. I leaned on the other door and stretched out my legs, crowding his. He kicked me. I kicked him back, but softly, kind of deniably, so as not to infuriate him—I knew better than that—but only to irritate. It bothered him when I moved, so I moved a lot. And I flicked my hair around as much as possible. This really sent him up.

Nigel turned around and looked at us in the dark. We were still and silent. He turned back.

I stretched noisily and shook my head again and then remembered where I was and who this guy was next to me. No, Louis is the hothead, I told myself. The reports are unanimous. This one is cold as ice. You cannot goad him, you can only pay him to kill, and even then, you need incontrovertible proof. He had been quite still for some time, with no hissing, so I flicked my hair again, defying my good sense.

Mack grabbed a handful of hair at the back of my head and yanked me down into the seat.

At that moment, Louis knocked on the window and Charlie started the car. Mack let go of my hair and I sat up in a hurry. Teague left Diane's apartment. Steve had an appointment with her at the SCIF immediately. I took the driver's seat in the heap and drove him there while the others went back to the safehouse in the Mercedes. Nigel drove the Jag in mechanically imposed radio silence.

I mulled over whether there would be consequences to my pointing a chair and whip at Mack when Steve came out of the SCIF and took the wheel for the ride home. He started in on me right away. First, he ragged me once again about the whole Louis thing, calling it unprofessional and out of bounds. What are the bounds of professionalism in the killing game, I wondered out loud. Raping your babysitter over a nickname? Is there a code of ethics? Thou wilt not consensually sleep with a specialist, only help him in a firefight? Did Steve have that written on a stone tablet somewhere? Steve had an answer. He always had an answer. Whatever caused failure, he said. Whatever impeded them or threatened them. He looked at me with those melty brown eyes empty of any warm thing, like a glass-eyed teddy bear. Thou shalt not endanger us, was the core of his philosophy.

"Look, Steve," I said finally, keeping my voice as steady as I could. "I've had all I can stand of double standards. I work within the parameters of my personality, just like you and everybody else. You make allowances for the oddities of every male you come into professional contact with, but somehow, I'm supposed to be made of molded plastic like a Barbie doll, both body and soul, no word, no gesture, no thought out of place. It's time you gave me the same breaks you would give a man not made of marble. Quit trying to prove through me that a woman can't do this job. It's not true."

"Of course, a woman can do this job, Barb," he said. "That's not the question. The question is, should she?"

"I think I've contributed. The team is still intact."

"True." He was silent for a moment. "Only just. But you create as many problems as you solve. Maybe the question is not whether another woman should but whether you should."

I smarted at that comment too much to trust myself with an answer.

"You know, Barb, your personality is in the way here. It's not just me and Charlie. Mack can't stand you. That's not healthy, or didn't you know that?"

I grunted and he kept on.

"You are up to your neck in the disintegration of a life-time relationship. You're more deeply mired in it than you have any right to be. You have been here less than two days, and already you're acting without any real understanding, least of all of what those two are capable of doing to you.

Charlie and I are minor league in comparison. Alex knew more, understood more when she met them years ago and she wound up badly hurt, more than even I realized if what you say is true. I'm wondering what's going to happen to you?"

"You're such a comfort, Steve."

We pulled up to the house in silence.

…

I slipped into the safehouse as unobtrusively as I could, staying as still as a flag on the moon with every step, hoping like hell Mack had forgotten about me.

No such luck.

EIGHTEEN

It began when I tried to tell Nigel I needed sleep, asking him as a colleague if he would cover me for the span of forty winks. We were all in the kitchen under bright ceiling lights that made my eyes stream. Nigel stood on my right. I sensed rather than saw Mack step behind me and to my left.

I guess my hair swung when I turned. I guess it hit Mack. I guess he caught it. I saw the light reflected in his knife, my throat held stiff by the grip he had on my hair, and I was sure this was the big It. The next moment, I wished it had been.

Without a sound but for the noise of sheering in my head, a sound from my private nightmares, his knife glided through my hair without effort. That was how sharp he kept it. One swipe, from crown to nape, leaving a four-inch-wide swath no more than an inch long. A curtain of once waist-long hair fell around my feet.

Nobody moved for a long time, or maybe time just halt-ed for a while. I don't know. I was busy crying, silently. Steve, Charlie, and Nigel stood looking at me and Mack, risking only an occasional surreptitious glance at Louis.

My silent tears dropped into the hair on the floor.

"*S… sie…*" Mack pointed the knife at me, but only to point.

I watched his face redden. He was not threatening me. He wasn't even talking to me. He was talking to Louis.

"*Sie. Ist. Ein. Engel,*" said Louis. The reference to a past event became more clear in his next sarcastic sentence. "You wanted her for yourself. This is a betrayal of me!"

Louis folded his arms and stood defiant, matching fury for fury.

"That is not …" Before leaving the room, Mack cleared the counter, creating a cascade of pans, dishes, cutlery, and assorted leftovers to the floor in a succession of smashing booms. A jar of coffee broke and scattered its contents to mingle with my late hair.

I lowered my head, letting the tears fall into the mess at my feet. They came faster, and a gasp, not quite a sob, escaped me. A finger under my chin gently lifted my face.

"Come," said Louis. "You need sleep." He took my arm and led me past the three men still standing dumbfounded in the kitchen.

I remember Nigel stepping aside, but the rest was a blur until Louis tucked the covers around me and kissed my forehead.

"In the morning, I will cut your hair properly," he said. "It will look beautiful. You will see."

"No. You can't." Impossibility had become a very real part of my life, "You will be dead. Diane will program the device for Cú Chulainn and then he will kill her, and you will kill him, and Mack will kill you."

He put a finger to my lips. "Go to sleep."

I touched the back of my head. Louis pulled my hand away and I fell asleep.

I had a nightmare that my hair had been cut.

Morning came three hours later. Louis did a tolerable job with the scissors and I tried to look appreciative.

I could feel he was uncomfortable. He worked in an awkward silence. His introductory belligerence that first night was preferable to this, so I thought I'd loosen up the conversation, or more accurately, lack of conversation. Besides, it would stop the snip-snip reverberating through my head.

"So what happened when you kissed her?" I asked a violent man wielding a sharp implement near the nape of my neck.

"I do not want to discuss it," he said. "It is between Misha and me."

"But it began as something between Alex and you."

"I told you …"

"I know, I know. It was about power. You hated her. You were angry. No doubt."

"Yes. It began that way."

"How did it end?"

He faced me, jaw tight, scissors pointed at my nose.

"You are angry with me right now," I said quietly. "Will you rape me, too?"

"Certainly not." He spat the words.

"So how did the kiss end?"

He was getting a little savage with those scissors, but so far only my hair seemed to be suffering.

A great mass of chocolate brown hair fell into my lap before he spoke. "I relented," he said. "Then she relented. Then she said no."

"And you stopped."

I waited.

"Yes. I began angry. I wanted to have my chance with her," he said after a long pause and the removal of a long piece of another swath of my hair. "Everybody has tried, even Charlie. I was never able to. I wanted to see...."

I waited some time, filing away this factoid concerning Charlie, then prompted, "And?"

"She liked the kiss. I could tell. But she said no."

Another long silence before he decided how to tell me what the fuck this was all about.

"Misha knew immediately. Within an hour. She could not hide the fact of the kiss or that she liked it. Most people are transparent to Misha. Alex's mind is completely naked before him and she feels guilt about everything. If she takes the last biscuit she considers herself selfish. We were about to climb into the jet to come here. He saw her guilt, she dropped her eyes, stammered, and trembled."

Louis ran his fingers through his hair and began work on another section of my head, this one around an ear.

"Alex is terrified of Misha," he said. "She has always been so. She loves him, yes, but he frightens her. He frightens most people. They think I am too jolly to be very dangerous, but I am the hasty one, not Misha. She knows he would not hurt her. She knows it here." He pointed to my head, then to his gut. "But here, when he looked at her, she turned to melting snow."

"You told him you raped her to protect her?"

"Yes. No." He yanked away a cut section of my hair savagely. "We did not have time for explanations. There is no room for any complication that does not belong to the operation. We were leaving. We always know we may not live. I did not want him to leave angry with her." Then in a softer voice, "Or for her to wait for him fearing his return."

Until then it was about great sex. At that moment, I fell in love.

"So you told him it was rape so that he would be mad at you and forgive her before he got on the airplane," I said.

"Yes. Even when there is nothing to forgive, such things can take time and assurance, and we did not have those. She did not have them. The kiss was my fault. I could give her this much at least. Also, I was angry with him for being so damned lucky to have her. It was a good way to hurt him. I thought I would explain privately to him when we got here. But he went mad. You saw him. Michael and Steve have kept me alive and now Misha is the unreliable one. It seems maybe it was too good a way to hurt him."

"He knows how lucky he is," I said. "You reminded him how easily such luck is lost. You have to tell him the truth, all of it. Somehow. I might be able to help you wordsmith it, but it will be up to you to say it."

"I do not think the smithing of words will be possible in the time he will allow me to speak," said Louis.

Charlie came in, cutting down the time I could glory in the sad triumph of being right, and I rushed to finish getting dressed. I wore black, like Nigel and the team, but I like to think my turtleneck and clean pair of jeans fit me better. Before I found my jacket, Charlie held me by my shoulders and searched my face.

"How are you?" he said.

Annoyed, was what I wanted to say, and more than a little nervous when you hold me that way.

"Fine," I answered not forgetting what he would have done to this particular disrupting influence.

"You are going to help Louis get away today, right?" He was in earnest. I could see it in those ice-blue eyes. So now he welcomed my disruption? I did not voice this. I did not want to remind him of what he previously thought should be done about me.

I looked at Louis. He stood next to a tall dresser, with one arm on the top, the other in his pants pocket. He seemed to doubt the younger man. "Michael," he said, "what makes you think I want to get away?"

Charlie let me go and faced him. "You've got a chance. I am giving you a chance. You can go solo; her government will help you."

I wasn't so sure about that last part, but I nodded anyway.

Louis played with some coins on top of the dresser.

"I would not last two weeks solo, Michael. I have no judgment. It is your father who has kept us alive until now."

"Give him time to cool down."

"He will not cool down. He will not forgive me."

Charlie bit his lip.

"Alex forgave you," he said. "Papa will, too."

"Alex is a saint," Louis sneered. He picked up two coins and laid them flat again.

"Give him a chance, please, Louis," said Charlie, then in a whisper, "for me?"

Louis studied the coins, glanced at Charlie, sighed, and nodded. "What is your plan?"

As plans go, it was pretty straightforward. I was to move the Jaguar to a spot near the back of the house, hide it in the brush, and wait for Louis there. Charlie made sure I understood it thoroughly and threatened me pretty convincingly if I didn't do as I was told.

After he left the room, I broached again the subject that had occurred to me while I watched Louis's depressed fingering of the coins. He stood with both hands in his pockets now, leaning on that dresser, watching his toe draw circles on the carpet before him.

"You must talk to him," I said.

"He will not listen to me." It seemed more than depression; it was despair.

"He will listen to me," I said, sounding more confident than I felt.

"Barbara, I need to talk to you," Nigel shouted from down the hallway.

Louis caught my arm before I reached the door.

"I am changing Michael's plan," he whispered. "Leave the car and the keys and get away. You must not be near when Misha catches me."

NINETEEN

Nigel hauled me outside through the front door the moment I came downstairs. He led me around the side of the house and through the brush into the stable block. We stepped over rotting planks and dusty loose bricks into a roofless room filled with rotting harnesses. A taller version of Nigel stood there, a bit more fit and with a lesser thickening in the middle suggesting he was only ever so slightly off his game, which was remarkable considering the amount of grey creeping up from his temples. He wore jeans and a sweatshirt and a relaxed upper-class manner that only the British can master.

"This is Stan," said Nigel. "He's SAS."

"Ex-SAS," corrected Stan. "I'm retired. Now I run a school library." Stan's dark eyes conveyed a wry look that matched his half-smile.

"Stan's going to help us get that detonator," said Nigel. "He's got the experience we need, what with being SAS."

"Ex, Nigel," said Stan. "I told you I never saw combat. The timing wasn't right in my career. Too much peace, don't you know? The IRA is pretty formidable, but I was never posted …"

Before Stan could finish his resume I asked him, "What do you know about Nigel's plan?"

"I know he hopes to steal a gadget from some guys who want to sell it to the IRA."

I looked at Nigel. "You told him about this op?"

"He's cleared. He is SAS."

"Was!" Stan and I said it simultaneously.

"Well, I trust him," said Nigel with an infatuated look in his eyes that told me he was besotted. Stan blushed.

"Nigel," I said slowly and clearly, "if I gave a retired special forces *general* compartmented information, I'd be shipped off to a listening post in an igloo on the Bering Strait. What the fuck do you think you're doing? We're in an op! We're live! But now who knows for how long?"

Nigel began sputtering.

"No, you listen Nigel. Whatever your government may think about this breach, mine expects me to report it, and both governments are fucking sieves so when it gets back to you know who, there is no corner of the world where we can be posted that will be out of range. Have you noticed my haircut, Nigel?"

Stan shuffled and said something along the lines of, um, very… interesting.

But I was in mid-rant and not to be deterred. "You were there when I got this haircut, Nigel, just a few hours ago. Have you forgotten how that knife went through all that thick hair like soft butter? Have you forgotten the look on his face?"

Nigel stood stupefied, but Stan picked it up right away. "Are you saying Nigel's in danger?"

"Yes," I told Stan. "And the guy he wants to steal the device from is the one who gave me the haircut."

"Not from them," said Nigel, "from the IRA."

"Because the IRA is also a bunch of really nice guys?" I looked at Stan and could see he was worried. He looked at Nigel full of concern. It turned to outright alarm as Nigel outlined his plan, born out of too many suspense movies.

"What I thought was I will leave the assembly point early," he told Stan, "meet up with you at the team's car. Then you and I and any others from your old firm who will join us —patriotic duty and all that—will pile into the car and drive it at top speed into this bow window at the front of the cottage. Surprise them, you see, with a big bang and all that. Then everybody jumps out of the car and sprays everything that moves in the cottage with automatic weapons fire, killing anybody who happens to be in our way. We grab the device and escape into the Jaguar. She," here he pointed at me, "will have moved it to the back of the house, unbe-knownst to the IRA or Charlemagne, you see."

We babysitters like to pretend we are not bloodthirsty.

I very nearly burst out laughing when I heard this. Stan stood blinking slowly and rubbed his chin.

"Nige," he said, "we need to talk about this. I keep telling you the career doesn't matter. They're going to screw you over and nothing you can do will stop it. I want you alive, Nige. Forget the damned job!"

"They?" I asked. "Who's they?"

"His governors," said Stan. He gave me a measuring look and decided I looked trustworthy. "They know."

"So the lousy safehouse, the security breaches …" And, unspoken, my doomed dangle.

"Stress," said Stan. "And sabotage. They wouldn't let him have a decent safehouse and told him it was the only one in the area, take it or leave it. He's for it, and he knows it. Look at him."

Nigel could have been mistaken for a statue if he hadn't been shaking so much.

"Yeah, well," I told Stan, "the words 'for it' will have a lot more meaning if this gets back to the team. Being a danger to them is unhealthy."

Stan raised his forearms, palms up, "Any suggestions?"

I bit my lip. "I have a meeting in twenty minutes. Give me a phone number where I can reach you in an hour. Take him with you." I pointed my chin at Nigel.

"You can't," said Nigel. "You can't just leave. I can't just leave. Not today."

"We'll both be here for the op. Go get some coffee or tea or whatever it is you Brits drink to stop the heebie-jeebies."

At that moment, a cask of whiskey would not have been enough for me.

Taking me aside, Stan sheepishly assured me he could talk Nigel out of it. He had his work cut out for him if he was going to keep his partner alive.

TWENTY

Here was the plan.

No, I take that back. Here were the plans. I knew four of them and suspected two more, for a total of six. That may be all there were, but I was still not completely sure of my plan.

The official plan, the one briefed by Nigel and Mack before lunch, was this:

Teague wanted the programming and demonstration to take place at his house at three o'clock that afternoon. He needed the remaining daylight to make use of the security advantage long, clear fenland vistas around the cottage gave him.

We gave Rutherford a story to tell him of the many precautions she had taken for her protection, but it was a lie, designed to look like a lie. We wanted him to think she was on her own, unattached to any trap.

While I was having my nap and nightmare in the wee hours, Louis had gone out to Teague's house and put his own touch in place. The device he set was undetectable until activated and would not be turned on until just before the actual demonstration. There was always a chance Teague might do a last-minute sweep. I thought the team's more sophisticated tap should have been there all along. I was sure we had missed something vital.

Teague lived in a charming, old thatched cottage set in a tract of open fields outlined by hedgerows and dotted with isolated stands of brush and low trees. These were good enough to hide in but getting to them across the fields meant total exposure.

A hundred yards from the house, an octagonal World War II pillbox stood obscured by bushes in an overgrown hedgerow. It was approachable, if one stayed low, through a ditch from a road a quarter mile behind. It measured eight feet in diameter and boasted an excellent, though screened, view of the approaches to the house.

We would watch and listen from there until Cú Chulainn's arrival, at which time the team would move in. Nigel and I would then position the team's car on an access road leading onto the nearby dual carriageway and wait for them there. He had a cleanup crew standing by, he assured me. Once Charlemagne was gone, we would proceed to the house in Nigel's Jaguar for the mopping up.

"We have intelligence of six IRA operatives in the area," Nigel told us. "Three are confirmed, and three are strongly suspected probabilities. They arrived yesterday. One of those confirmed is a sniper."

"So seven with Teague, eight with Cú Chulainn," said Charlie.

"Unless Cú Chulainn is one of the six," said Steve.

There followed an internal discussion about the sniper, mainly between father and son.

Something niggled at me when I heard this ordinary conversation. It wasn't the odds. Bad odds were part of the business. It was the assumption that Cú Chulainn would be a threat, a fighting threat. I suppose it arose from the fact that the late explosives expert of the team, Vasily Sobieski, had also been a martial artist capable of killing a man bare-handed. But on the teams I had encountered, the explosives expert was usually the softest member. I began to re-examine all my assumptions.

Nigel ended the briefing with special instructions: if possible, incapacitate but do not kill Cú Chulainn. We understand this is not likely, but in any event, please try to leave at least one of his people alive. Thank you. Payment terms and procedures standard.

Charlie's plan: while Nigel moved Charlemagne's car, I was to move the Jaguar to a twisting road on the side of the house and in sight of its back door, hide it behind a screen of trees that line the road, wait for Louis to join me there and then drive like hell to the base.

Louis's plan: I was not, under any circumstances, to wait for him. I suspected he did not intend to survive.

Mack's plan: I had no way of knowing what his plan was, but I deduced that he intended to shoot Louis immediately after killing Cú Chulainn. Mack would forgo using the knife this time, I thought, in the interests of efficiency and perhaps a lifetime of friendship, not to mention the real probability Louis knew perfectly well how to defend against a knife attack, even Mack's.

Steve's plan: this is another conjecture, but an educated one. Steve would make sure Louis didn't run out the back door.

My plan: I would wait in the Jaguar for Louis. I would drive him myself as Charlie had instructed, and I had already begun to arrange the transportation needed to get him out of the country. I had a few other contingencies in play as well.

Teague's plan: I figured he would shoot Diane the moment Cú Chulainn was satisfied with the device. I noticed none of the plans, including my own, made any provision for the possibility that he might shoot her before this. I began revision number one thousand and one to my plan.

As it turned out, what happened was none of the above.

TWENTY-ONE

We had been in that pillbox for two and a half hours, after positioning ourselves well ahead of any of Cú Chulainn's pickets, when Diane blew the whole operation.

I was spending plenty of time feeling exposed. My neck stretched upward like a chicken's gullet under an axe. Back in the days when I had hair, I would have worn it up anyway, but in a breezy World War II pillbox surrounded by specialists, I missed it desperately. No, that's not true. I was indeed surrounded by specialists and my hair was not there to protect me, that much was true, but the only one who bothered me was the one with the knife. I had felt that blade once. Well, my hair felt it. I did not want my throat to feel it too. I swallowed a lot, telegraphing a giant tell as to what I was thinking.

It was drizzling outside and damp inside. A thin slurry of mud covered the concrete floor. We had been standing the entire time. Everybody— except Mack, of course—shivered visibly at least once. I shivered a lot more than that, and not always from the cold and damp. Another tell.

Louis turned on the transmitter he had placed in Keegan's cottage. It was neither too early nor too late, so reception was perfect. Diane arrived a little before three and may have meant her conversation for Keegan alone, but she had a large and varied audience a hundred yards away and according to our intelligence, an even larger contingent inside the house.

"I had an old house like this before I took command of the squadron and moved on base," she said. "It had mice. In the kitchen. Hordes of them."

"What did you do about them?" said Teague. You could hear the distraction and boredom in his voice. He was watching for Cú Chulainn.

"I set traps for them." She paused. "I caught six of them one day. I would trap one and the bait would be gone. I figured dead mice don't eat cheese, so I reset it each time with fresh bait. I wondered if the mice had a black lottery going on down in the hole somewhere, drawing straws to see who would go next so the rest could eat."

"What the hell is she on about?" It was Nigel who said it, but we were all thinking it.

"She's warning him," I said. For the best of motives, I might have added. Now she would have the opportunity to watch her Dr. Jekyll become Mr. Hyde.

It did not take Keegan long to swallow his special potion. He began to sound alert, opening with some pointed questions for which, of course, she had no answers. We listened in silent tension.

"Let go!" Diane's voice rang with panic.

"She's blown it. I'll kill her," said Nigel.

He got the look he deserved from all of us.

I realized Mack was looking at me without love and affection. He was irritated that I existed, and no doubt figured rightly I had a plan to thwart him in his desire to kill Louis. This was my moment to put my plan into action. He looked ready to shoot me on the spot anyway, so I carried out one of my more outrageous contingency plans by stepping right up to him. I hoped his reaction would be hampered by the HK he had slung on his shoulder, making the plan a tad on the happy side of plausible. I put my arms around his neck and kissed him. On the mouth. I tried to make it sensuous and alluring but there are just some occasions in a woman's life when that's out of reach, like when she's kissing an unwilling half-crazed specialist with the adrenaline rising in his blood, so I kept it brief.

"That's what he did," I said, stepping back. "That's all he did. She said no, and he stopped." Sometimes a visual aid is more powerful than a lot of words. I sincerely hoped so.

Nigel gaped. Steve and Charlie exchanged a glance.

I figured I'd leave it up to Louis to explain all that stuff about Alex's fear of him being mixed with fear for him if and when he got home, assuming my gambit worked, and Louis lived.

Mack looked at Louis behind me.

"You were right as usual," said Louis in an exasperated voice. "I was angry with you. It was the best way to hurt you, but not to betray you. I am sorry."

Mack swung the HK off his shoulder. I closed my eyes and did not see him hand it to Charlie. When there was no firing, I opened my eyes and Mack was right there before me. In the next instant, his arms encircled me like a vise, and he kissed me, thoroughly, with plenty of tongue and a hand on my bottom. I must confess I was not unwilling by the end of that kiss and he knew it.

He broke it off, stepped back, and looked at Louis, now only a step or two behind me. "So, we are even," said Mack. "Come. Let us go." He took the HK from Charlie and led the way out.

"No!" said Nigel. "You can't! Cú Chulainn isn't there yet. Stop! Come back!"

I kept a steady watch through binoculars as the team made its way crouching along the hedgerow to a small copse behind the cottage. There was still no sign of a car that might contain our quarry.

Nigel sputtered and complained, then ran out of the pillbox, absconding quickly while mumbling about the Mercedes. He waived the key he thought he had as evidence of his intention.

The Mercedes pulled up to the front of the cottage just after he left. My private army got out. Stan skulked to the corner of the house and began firing an M-16 I had managed to pick up from the Resident. Mace got out of the driver's side, strolled to the front door, pounded on it with both fists and forearms and screamed, "Diane, get your ass out here!"

The door opened with a shudder; she ran out and Mace threw her on the ground, covering her with his body as gravel spurted like a fountain all around them. He rolled them both against the wall directly under the sniper, who redirected his fire toward Stan.

I put down the binoculars and ran to the Jaguar, for which I did have the key. I followed Charlie's plan anyway, thinking even if Louis was out of the woods, it would be good to have transportation close by that house. Besides, if Louis was still in danger, I did not want to risk Louis's life and my own by disobeying Charlie.

After the op, I listened to the tape of what happened in the cottage. Diane kept to her script and did not compound her initial mistake. She programmed the device under considerable duress but without a word about me, Steve, or the Resident. When the pounding on the door began, Teague swore and must have loosened his hold just enough for her to break free to make an exit under cover of the noise coming from two directions, followed in two seconds by even more noise as the team entered.

TWENTY-TWO

I t would be easier to count the things that went right in the plan, or I should say gaggle of plans, which turned into a cluster fuck.

Change of Plan Number Infinity: my hiding place for the Jaguar was already occupied by a white Ford. I had to drive on and look for another spot, which I found around a bend in the road further up. I scrambled back along a ditch crouching low and hid myself in the hedgerow at the rendezvous point where I was to meet Louis if things did not go well for him.

I was in a good position to see him coming from the house, which is why I could see a figure slipping along another ditch not far from the Ford. The figure came closer, heading for the other car. This was not Louis. This was a short female. I watched her from my hiding place. My reassessment of assumptions had told me who she was. She was at the pub that night. I remembered her sharp perusal of the bar. Now I had confirmation. She carried the cigar box I knew contained the detonator with its battery.

Fiona climbed out of the ditch and ran for the Ford. Of course, I had been ready to fire but was not quick enough. I collected myself and ran onto the road firing at the white car as it bore down on me. To tell the truth, I fired at the wrong side. It was a British car after all. I did manage to blow out the windshield in a spectacular shower of glass. The car swerved a bit, not to miss me, but because Cú Chulainn was thrown off balance. She righted herself quickly and hit the gas.

I ran after her like that was going to do any good and reached the Jaguar in time to see the Ford negotiate a curve at top speed almost half a mile away by road. The route over the fields, cutting the curves, was shorter. So I took it. Actually, there was no route over the fields. I made one.

What I gained in directness of travel I partly lost in speed. I made one, well a few, doughnuts in the mud, but all in all I made good progress in getting behind my quarry. I was only a quarter mile back when I reached the road. The Jaguar's superior twelve cylinders took over from there.

I spun out on a sharp left curve and put that incredible machine back on the road by way of a ditch. What a car! But now I was almost half a mile behind again.

Cú Chulainn's Ford was no match for the Jaguar. I behaved myself on the curves now and gained on her again. I was just about to close the final gap when the road ended in a T-intersection. Cú Chulainn turned left. It was not a bad turn, considering her speed, but though she was fast, the truck coming from the right was faster. It climbed up the back of the Ford as if it were a ramp truck. But it wasn't of course, and it flattened with a pop. I was relieved to see the truck driver scramble out just before the explosion that could not have come solely from the gas in the Ford's tank.

I noticed a tire was rubbing the Jag's fender as I sped back to Planned Hiding Place Number One where I heard a few pops of a dying gun battle and a final boom from what had to be a sniper rifle. Then, silence.

Sinking despair. Rising panic.

I screeched back onto the road and raced to the team rendezvous. Nobody there. I punched it the few hundred yards back to the driveway of the cottage, screeched through the turn, and pulled up beside the Mercedes where Mace and Stan had left it. Nigel stood a few feet ahead, arms folded, a large welt on his left temple. The team was moving toward him from Teague's house. Something was wrong. One of them was being half carried, half dragged toward us.

"Where is the ambulance?" demanded Mack.

The fool shrugged.

Mack shoved him when he was close enough but could not wipe the insolent glare from Nigel's eyes.

"You blew it," said Nigel.

There were more demands for an agreed-upon ambulance. Nigel stonewalled. Mack and Charlie checked the Mercedes for alarms. This was an exercise in futility, given Stan and Mace's recent use of it, but good habits save lives. Louis supported Steve, who clutched a bloody spot on his abdomen.

"Why must you be such a bullet magnet?" said Louis.

"Why do I have to go in first all the time?" Steve said, gasping.

They laid him across the backseat. Louis rummaged in the trunk.

"Did you leave one alive?" Nigel demanded of Mack, ignoring the fury on his face. "Did you do that at least? Did you get any leads?"

"We know who is Cú Chulainn. If you will not provide an ambulance, at least give us a doctor to travel with us. We will send him back when ours can take over."

"If you know who he is, then go after him for bloody Christ's sake!" Nigel's enraged fleshy face wobbled like red jelly.

I was watching the utter self-destruction of a former professional, and it was not pretty. The contrast with Mack's cool rationality was sobering.

"Some other time," Mack said as he turned away.

Louis shouted at me from the car. He was stooping in the open back door, holding Steve's shoulders.

"Hold his legs!"

I did as directed. Steve began to vomit, the spasms intensifying his pain to increasingly unbearable levels. Charlie took over Louis's position at the head so Louis could measure a dose of morphine he had taken from a satchel in the trunk. The fact that Steve was being given morphine while still operational meant it was serious.

Louis shoved the needle into an arm, and the retching eased, then stopped. Steve relaxed, but I kept one hand on an ankle while I reached for the car phone on the console.

I caught Mack's eye as he leaned in the front door and reached for a separate radio mike.

"Where's your airplane?" I asked.

He told me. I told him to move it to the air base at Alconbury and started dialing from the carphone while he barked into the radio.

The Resident answered my call himself. I don't think I blew his identity, as if that were even important at the moment because everybody was talking at once and nobody had time to pay attention except for the nearly unconscious Steve. Nigel still sulked by the Jaguar obstructing the team's progress, but not making any progress of his own, so he was equally oblivious to my calling our resident on a clear line.

Anyway, I was prepared to blow the Res's identity and smash a host of flash instructions just to keep the self-destructing basket case busy while I got the team out of there.

"An escort will meet you at the Alconbury gate," I told Mack. "They'll lead you to the flightline and a flight surgeon will meet you there."

Mack pointed his chin at the short round babysitter, clucking and moaning with tears in his eyes as he ran a hand over the Jaguar's roof and bonnet.

"What if he closes the airways?" said Mack.

"I'll take care of him. You go. Now."

It did not occur to me that Mack might not trust me, so I was mystified at first by his transient hesitation. Then I remembered all the events of the past two days that had been squeezed out of my mind under the pressure of havoc. I had only one goal at this moment: to protect my team. It took Mack a second to assure himself about my intention and then force himself to take an order from a woman.

Charlie sat in the muck that covered the back seat, Steve's head in his lap. Mack and Louis climbed into the front. They were gone before Nigel looked up from his inspection of the Jaguar.

"What the hell...?" he said as they sped away. "Where...?"

I shrugged. "Maybe they went after Cú Chulainn."

"Can you believe it?" Nigel was addressing a point somewhere to the left of my right ear. I turned quickly, but no one was there. He continued his address to an imaginary listener.

"They never failed before. For anybody. And when the day comes, they fail for me. Never missed a shot, and when they miss, it's got to be me. Fifteen years of fucking flawless precision, shattered when I need their top performance the most. Unbelievable. Un-fucking-believable."

He went on for a long time, in pretty much the same words, liberally punctuated by words like 'me' and 'fucking'.

I interrupted on the third iteration.

"Nigel, do you have a cleanup crew standing by? Don't you think it's time we went into the house?"

"What in all hell happened to my car?"

I wasn't sure he was entirely there anymore. You would have thought the car was his vital appendage. It took precedence over Charlemagne. He never even tried to call his people to order an intercept or even to monitor them. There was a car phone in the Jag, which was now emitting a high-pitched whistle, but he did not look at it even once as he and I moved the car up to a position in front of the house that would not interfere with the cleanup crew. Nigel had taken success very well, but he was disintegrating under failure.

"How do we reach your cleanup crew, Nigel?"

"What did you do? Enter a fucking rally? What in hell am I supposed to tell my boss?"

"The cleanup crew, Nigel," I insisted as I stopped in front of the silent little house.

I dreaded everything, going in alone, going in with Nigel the Nut, going in with the clean-up crew, going in without them. Were Mace and even Diane alive? Louis's expression had given no hint. His concern was centered on Steve. Was that a good sign or a bad sign? The house's eerie stillness was not encouraging.

"There's a car wash in Huntingdon," said Nigel. "That will help."

I rubbed my eyes and pinched the bridge of my nose. It helped keep me from decking him. Screaming at him was still a possibility.

TWENTY-THREE

We approached the silent house and found four people. Three sat on the gravel driveway against the wall under a busted bow window. Teague's hands were behind his back. Stan stood over him pointing the M-16 at his chest. Mace and Diane completed the tableau, her head on the big man's chest. She appeared to be asleep. It was not yet four o'clock, but dusk came early in February. It was cold and drizzling and they were outside.

"They told us not to go in there," said Stan.

"So who the fuck is the target?" Nigel asked Diane.

She shook herself awake. "Target?"

"The voice. Whose voiceprint was it?"

She looked puzzled. I noticed, even in the gloom, that one eye was badly bruised and swollen almost shut.

"I… don't know," she said. "It was somebody British. With an accent, I mean."

Teague dropped his head and swung it from side to side. He had been about to kill her for her knowledge of the target.

Mace looked at me. "I didn't know," he said, "about Fiona, I mean."

"Not your fault. Thanks for doing what I asked."

I turned to Nigel. "We are going in there now," I ordered. "If the phone in there is working, I will call your crew for you. What is their number?"

"I know of another car wash in St. Ives if the Huntingdon one isn't working." He turned his head and looked at me for the first time. "It freezes up sometimes, you see."

"Yeah, sure. I see. Listen, Nigel, what do you say we ask your cleanup crew to give it a wash when they get here? Give me the number and I'll call them."

"Cleanup crew?"

"The one standing by. What's the number?"

He fumbled for his wallet.

"No, Nigel, it's in your head. Look for the number in your head."

He wrinkled his forehead and spewed out numbers. I wrote them down as they came, every one of them, praying one set would be the magic one.

"On second thought, Nigel, I'll go by myself. You help Stan guard the prisoner."

Stan took his arm while still covering Teague. I had to admit he knew what he was doing.

Nigel continued to sputter and resist Stan's life-saving restraint.

"Knock it off, Nigel," I said. "You owe this guy your life. Exercise some discretion for fuck's sake." To Stan, I said, "Our agreement holds. Whatever you have to do to muzzle him, do it. I heard nothing, never met you, have no idea what you were doing here. Thanks for helping my guy Mace save the colonel. I don't owe you, because we're even." I looked at Nigel. "Your career, such as it is, is still intact, Nigel. My silence is bought and paid for, but Stan is right. It's only a matter of time before your hierarchs find a way to jettison you in the most painful way possible. Don't give them the satisfaction. Settle down and have a nice life."

I went in through the front door.

I found the number for Nigel's cleanup crew on the fourth try down the list, using the phone at a quaint table seat in the very tiny, very English cottage's entry hall. As I hung up on the last call, I stood in silence, staring at three closed doors, a staircase, and one open door. The open door was the way outside next to me. I was tempted.

I had left it open so I could monitor Nigel as he muttered to Stan.

Professionally speaking, maybe I should have looked inside before calling for cleanup. I might have been in a better position to specify what we needed. But I took it for granted that Nigel had thought of everything back when he was still thinking and had planned accordingly. Whatever else he had been driven to become, he began as a top-rated intelligence officer and babysitter. I had to believe that when allowed to, he would do his job. His boss wouldn't know anything about cleanup crews.

Also, I had an overwhelming urge to procrastinate. Can't think why.

With the crew on the way and Nigel busy muttering about the car, I finally screwed up the discipline to open door number one. It was the kitchen. Very charming. Nothing amiss. Door number two turned out to be the dining room, all in perfect order.

I chided myself for my cowardice as I put my hand on the last door handle. Please don't make me climb the stairs, I thought. I was sure that amount of creepy would be too much. I took a deep breath.

It's a very good thing I held my breath initially. Had I walked in breathing, I would have tossed the breakfast I had not eaten. Of course, there was blood everywhere. I've seen lots of scenes, many of them worse, but this one had tied itself to me. It was a serpent coiling tightly around my ankles and I could not dance enough to shake it off, but I did jump involuntarily. Again, I was glad I had skipped breakfast.

The small lounge was stuffed with easy chairs, a two-seater sofa, rug, overturned coffee table, television, and three bodies with AKs still in their hands. The usual. The fireplace had been walled in and now sported a two-burner gas heater. Flowers and songbirds papered the wall. A dead man lay in front of the gas heater. He showed signs, or rather wounds, that suggested he'd not gone down fighting. He went down talking. It was amazing how much blood a human body holds.

I climbed the stairs because I had to. At the top was a little room over the front door that the British call a box room. It had been used as a sniper perch. Empty shells littered the floor. A rifle with a decent scope on it still ticked as its heat cooled. A movement on my left made my head jerk around again. I moved a chair to investigate. The man was still alive, but barely, and obviously in considerable pain. He seemed to be dying, but that did not mean he could not be dangerous. I was not ready to let him take me with him. Another body lay, quite dead, behind the sniper rifle.

"There is an ambulance outside," I said to the man still living as I checked him for weapons. "I'll have them give you something for the pain."

"Don't count on it, lass," he said.

"Just tell them what they want to know," I said, "and tell them quickly."

His face set in defiance.

"Look," I said, "we already know who she is, or was. Don't suffer for nothing. Just tell them."

I worried as he closed his eyes that he would not live to say anything. I did not want to be debriefed. Between Teague and this guy, the facts could easily be established without my information. My involvement would only raise questions, primarily about me.

The cleanup crew had arrived and were lifting the bloodless corpse from behind the rifle.

"That's not Mack's mark," said a voice behind me.

I jumped even as I recognized the accent of my raving colleague and looked at him carefully. His face had become thoughtful. Sane? To be determined.

"Who else uses a knife?" I wondered.

"None of the others that we know, but Mack didn't do that."

"Why?"

He shrugged.

"It looks like his mark." I tried not to make it sound like a challenge. "It looks just like the examples in the file."

He stared at me a moment. "I know. But the ones I've seen were not in any file. And this is not like them. The one in the lounge is his, though, and two watchers on the approach and in the brush out back."

"What's different with this one?"

He shrugged again.

"Then yours is a theory," I said.

"No. Worse. An intuition."

He looked at me through bleary eyes that swam in the fatigue and despair that filled the sockets. Behind those eyes, Nigel had returned to reality. I still did not like him, but it was good to have him back.

...

Louis later briefed me regarding the action in the house. Mack was running point as usual. He had taken out two watchers in the brush on the approach to the house and was about to enter the cottage to look for the sniper when chaos and gunfire boomed from the front of the building. A woman ran out the back door toward a small copse to the left. They could not see if she carried anything because of the angle at which she ran. There was automatic rifle fire to the right front, and the boom of an unsuppressed sniper rifle at the front center, evidently upstairs or in an attic, but nothing was coming their way.

Mack led the way in through the kitchen door, directed Charlie and Steve upstairs to take care of the sniper, and proceeded through the lounge and out a side window to take out the automatic rifle outside. Louis covered him in this effort, killing two. Charlie and Steve came downstairs into a fierce battle with Keegan and two others firing at Louis. One of their rounds hit Steve. He, Charlie, and Louis managed to kill one and take Teague and one other as prisoners. Mack returned and conducted an interview with the other man to gain the identity of Cú Chulainn and then dispatched him.

They left Teague alive per Nigel's request, taking him outside to the corner of the house where a man continued to fire an M-16 into the air. He stopped firing when he saw the knife blade before his face. Louis took the rifle but returned it when Mack ordered that the prisoner be turned over to this man.

Stan had handcuffs with him. *Is this something you learn in SAS school?* He secured Teague's hands behind his back and led him to the front of the house. The team went back inside briefly to make it safe. One was alive upstairs, but not for long. Charlie disarmed him and rendered the sniper's rifle unusable, not that the dying man would ever have been capable of getting to it.

The reason I had this last bit of information is because of the discussion Louis related between father and son when Charlie came back downstairs. Mack was sharp with his criticism of leaving a man within reach of a weapon, no matter how wounded, no matter how short a time, especially when, given the layout of the place, the man would inevitably be at his back. Charlie took the rebuke like a stone, Louis told me.

By then Steve's injury was asserting itself and Louis had to half carry him outside.

The entire action had taken a little under four minutes.

TWENTY-FOUR

I had plenty of reasons to resign. Pick one.

The thrill was gone.
I reached the finish line but lost the race.
Personal problems.
To spend more time with my family.
A reassessment of my life.
Identity crisis.
My health.
I couldn't hack it.

That last one is no more true than any of the others but the men in my section would have picked it and they would be wrong.

I resigned because I had fallen in love with a killer and there were two things I could not bear: the thought of seeing another example of his work and zipping him into a body bag like the bags I had seen zipped in that English cottage.

There were contributing factors. I was more of a pariah than Steve had ever been, even though no one knew about my part in Cú Chulainn's death. The Section seemed mad at me for coming back alive.

The guy in the box room lived just long enough to tell Nigel who Fiona was. After persuasion, Teague corroborated the fact, so I was off the hook there.

Speaking of Steve, he deserves credit as one of the biggest contributors to my decision. The pain in those Teddy Bear eyes as he came out of the house and the muck he lay in with his head on Charlie's lap made me realize I could be on the same road Steve followed. I got the hell off it. So what if the only way off was in a ditch?

I re-defected to my old friends in the FBI and took a job in Miami, not too junior, but not as far up as I would have been had I stayed.

It was kind of nice to be Millie Aldrich again, all the time, and at home all the time.

I suppose.

I had two months to wait before starting the job and after setting up my new apartment near the beach, spent the rest of the delay back at my parents' farm in Nebraska.

My family put on a big picnic for the Fourth of July. They set up tables and chairs in the meadow that bordered the house where I grew up. Dad officiated the barbecue. My brothers and brothers-in-law cooked steaks for the adults and hot dogs for my nieces, nephews, thieving dogs, and the piglet one of those nephews was raising for 4H. Mom and my four sisters provided baked beans, coleslaw, three kinds of potato salad, six fruit salads, and apple, blueberry, and cherry pies.

I did nothing and enjoyed it thoroughly, sitting in a lawn chair drinking gin and tonic, disturbed only by an occasional badminton cock the wind blew my way. I was otherwise left alone to meditate upon the view.

The house and meadow are set at the top of a rise in the rolling Nebraska prairie. From my lawn chair, I could see for some distance along the winding dirt road leading to the farm and the house. I wondered vaguely who could be coming this way as I saw a glint of metal in a small dust cloud rolling toward us. The vision grew into a distinct shape and color. I stopped drinking when I thought the color was black and the shape a Mercedes. I stood up when, at a half mile, it turned a final bend and made me suspect I had been drinking too much.

"Now who could that be?" Ma stood at my elbow, genuinely curious.

I tried to hide my alarm. Not here, I thought, as if the road would lead anywhere else. *No. No. Don't come here.*

But they did.

And Ma was right there to greet them when they got out of the car. So was Dad. So was I, nervously. The four men wore lightweight suits which would never be light enough in that July sun. Charlie took off his tie almost immediately, but not his coat. Steve loosened his tie and also kept his coat on. He was pale, thinner than he had been five months before, but fit. Sunglasses hid Mack's royal blue eyes. I was glad. I did not want him to frighten my mother.

"You know each other from work?" said Ma. "How splendid! I don't think we've ever met anybody Millie works with."

I stumbled over introductions and my parents led the way back to the meadow. They were jolly beyond belief at the prospect of introducing a whole set of Millie's friends— all of them men!—to the family.

We ate. I watched Charlemagne watch each other's back as I navigated the conversation through torturous topics in which their answers were every bit as vague as my family's questions were pointed. They were in business, they said. What kind? In Europe. My brighter nephews caught on to this right away. They were themselves quite experienced at evading pointed questions from the family. Louis answered a few of my nephews' questions with a silent stare and they went off to play softball. *Bright boys.*

I worried about two teenaged nieces. Between them, they had glued four wistful eyes onto Charlie. Steve sat on a tree swing watching his back as Charlie leaned against the tree, beer in hand, a girl on either side, and a smile on his face. I remembered my lost wrestling bout with him, his words about my being a disruption, and the bloodless sniper. I found an excuse to call the girls over and direct them toward my aunt Jo who didn't need any help with the chili, but I pretended she did. When I turned back to my seat, Charlie was watching me, and the smile was gone.

My once lonely lawn chair became part of a crowd. Mack sat on my left, Louis on my right. Ma sat down next to Mack and tried to start a conversation. He was polite enough, I suppose. I was still fretting over my nieces and so found myself caught off guard when Louis made a loud announcement in French. He asked the assemblage if anybody spoke French. Blank smiles all around.

"*Bon*," he said to me. "I know this is very rude, but I want some privacy. You have quit your job."

I nodded and asked how things were with him, politely not mentioning that I was pleasantly surprised he was still alive.

"*Bien*," he said. An all-purpose word with a meaning that ranges from fantastic to good enough.

Now that he had dragged my attention to him, I had to discipline myself not to drink in every detail. I knew Mack would be watching and nothing would escape him. I forced my gaze away from Louis's black eyes from time to time in an effort, probably obvious, to hide the hammering my heart was doing in my chest.

"Nigel paid us finally," said Louis.

"Did he?"

Louis nodded and sipped his beer. "He refused at first, you know."

"I heard."

"Even before they identified Cú Chulainn, Nigel said he would not pay for an accidental death."

"Oh."

"Then they found a bullet in what remained of the body. Did you know Cú Chulainn had bled out, or so they think?" He arched an eyebrow at me.

"Oh?" I did not dare look him in the eye.

"We argued the bullet meant it was not an accident. Payable. Nigel sputtered about it not matching any of our weapons, but he paid in the end, just before he retired."

I sipped the last of my gin and tonic and contemplated the ice cubes in my glass.

"What I am wondering," said Louis, "is whether you are coming home to claim your share."

I watched Steve swinging slowly. He seemed relaxed, but I knew better.

"I'm flattered," I said, "but I can't."

He said nothing, but there was no smile. I still could not look at him directly, so I studied the ice in my glass as it melted.

Mack stirred. "Excuse me," he said to my mother to break off their one-sided non-conversation. Then to Louis, in French: "Barbara does not understand you."

Louis frowned at him.

"She thinks you are asking her to join the team."

Freaky mind reader.

Louis looked at me, puzzled. I found the courage to look at him and he chuckled.

"*Vraiment?*" he said. "Did you think…?"

I managed only the beginning w sound in well yes when he laughed in earnest.

"You a specialist?" he said. "You are barely competent as a babysitter!"

Even Mack allowed himself a short chuckle.

Thoroughly confused, I began to cry into my melting ice cubes when Louis stopped laughing, leaned over, and took my hand.

"No," he said, "not with us, with me. I am asking you to come home with me. Home to Vasily's Carpet. I ask poorly because I have never done this."

I was more confounded than ever.

"What about Diane?" I asked.

"She married her pilot." He wrinkled his brow and shrugged. "And she is not my type. You described her very well. She is quite beautiful, and it was good for us that you saved her life, but…." He gave me the smile that always makes me wonder what he's up to. "She is no lion tamer."

I didn't go with him right away. We stayed for pie.

I did ask the usual pertinent questions. Do you love me? He said he didn't know but he had never asked a woman to marry him before so that might be an indication, and also something about not being able to stop thinking about me and talking about me. Misha nodded wearily at the latter statement. I wondered if he was to be in on all our most romantic moments.

Eventually, my mother moved to the other side of Louis to force more non-conversation with him. Misha apologized for cutting my hair. Sort of. What I mean is, he said he was sorry he lost his temper but not sorry he cut my hair because he likes it better short.

I will never get used to him.

"I was to take out the sniper," he said in German. He did not check if anyone spoke German, because he knew no one did, damn him, the freak. But he continued, "I was diverted by someone firing an automatic rifle, an M-16, an American weapon. Someone we did not know. I was about to take him out. He was an older man with dark hair, not entirely fit, but more than competent with the rifle. He never heard me." He paused. "At the last moment, when my knife was poised, I realized he was firing into the air and drawing fire from the tangos."

"He had strict instructions not to endanger the team," I said.

He waited. I was going to have to confess.

"He was covering for the guy rescuing the dangle."

"You should have told me," said Misha pausing again. "Michael and Steve had to take out the sniper. A few weeks later, in April, I met this man I had almost killed. He is Nigel's lover. Nigel has retired at his insistence. We offered to meet with his superiors to do what we did for Steve to keep him from being dismissed, but Stan said it would not work. He is right of course, and Nigel would be difficult to work with now."

"Because he's gay?" I asked.

"Because he is no longer a good babysitter." He bored holes into me even through his sunglasses. "Good babysitters do not make private plans during our operations."

I will never know if he was referring to my rescue of the dangle or if he knew about Nigel's half-baked plan to steal the detonator. It was probably both and included my silence about the stupid plot and his egregious security breach. Misha's statement was both specific and ambiguous at the same time, a hallmark of his unique species of threats. One may be in doubt as to the complete meaning of what he says, but never about his intent in saying it. I shivered visibly.

"*Bon*, as Louis would say," he said with a half-smile, acknowledging my capitulation. "Make your goodbyes. We leave immediately."

…

As I dodge the daily snarls that animate life at Vasily's Carpet, I find I do have a first-class talent as a lion tamer, primarily because I have developed a profound awareness of their claws.

EPILOGUE

Buddy faced his second tribunal in less than two years. Gizmo and Bruno sat on either side of the chairman. Again.

The chairman, a political appointee, looked at the folder before him, striped with red tape and emblazoned with the word WEDGE. He seemed to have a recollection that he had seen it before, but this particular department of the organization was so incomprehensible to him, he had no mental framework upon which to hang the memory. He looked at the file knowing he did not want to open it. He was certain he would not like this hearing and he would leave it with no clearer understanding of what the hell these men were talking about than he had after the last time.

He thought about lunch instead.

Bruno opened the proceedings. "Buddy, we're here to discuss the fact that you've had a second babysitter join Charlemagne."

Charlemagne, mused the chairman, was the first Holy Roman Emperor, though he wasn't a Roman and probably not holy. *Sort of like these guys, a loose collection of is and is not.*

"Not *joined* the team, Bruno," said Buddy. "She married one of them. She didn't become operational. Except as a wife, I suppose."

The chairman wondered briefly if Charlemagne was somehow involved in childcare, but then reflected on the specialized jargon used by all departments in this organization and wisely kept his mouth shut.

"That's even worse," said Gizmo. "Pillow talk can lay everything bare." He frowned at his unfortunate phrasing.

The chairman was deciding which wine he wanted with lunch.

Buddy swiveled his froggy eyes at the ceiling before replying. "Gizmo, she was a senior babysitter. *The* senior babysitter. We have alerted her former team there is a possibility of a breach, but not a probability. Her team before that one was wiped out thanks to the bonehead who replaced her as their babysitter. I might add I had nothing to do with that selection. Her teams prior to them have all either disbanded or been blown to smithereens in various parts of the globe. It's not a long-lived profession."

"I don't think you can crow about your ability to select babysitters, Bud," said Bruno. "You've lost two in eighteen months to the same team."

The chairman was now certain they were not talking about childcare.

"I'll admit I made a mistake on the first one, but Millie was the right choice for this op. She saved everybody's ass out there. Even the cousins are pleased."

The chairman frowned. It sounded like they were referring to families again.

"Everybody's ass except the tangos," Buddy clarified.

Dancing families? The chairman contemplated a refreshing, crisp white wine to counter the morning's tedium.

"That explains why the cousins are happy," said Gizmo. "But you don't think it was a mistake to assign a woman to such a team? They have a reputation for being pretty brutal."

"No, Gizmo, I don't. I don't think a man would have been able to save the situation. From what I understand, brutal is an understatement in this case."

"So bottom line, you're saying the possibility of a breach is remote?"

"I'm saying exactly that," said Buddy. "She was a first-class agent and besides, she defected to the FBI before she accepted Charlemagne, so she's already been thoroughly debriefed."

Finally, something the chairman understood. He spent most of his days repairing the damage done by daily internecine battles waged by these subordinates. He and his FBI counterpart often joked the Soviets enjoyed more respect in their hallways than members of the sister services. The word 'defected' was a telling use of their peculiar language. The chairman's spirits briefly improved before being brought back down again by Bruno's next observation.

"Accepted them, Buddy? She didn't marry all of them, did she?"

"She married the Frenchman. But the dynamics of the team are such that she may as well have married all."

"Really?" The three members of the panel said it simultaneously. The chairman understood this point with no trouble at all.

"Minds out of the gutter, gentlemen," said Buddy. "I mean that except for what you're thinking about, she now lives in a cage with all of them and must deal accordingly. I have no doubt she will do so admirably."

The chairman took his dignity into his hands and ventured a brief question. "Did you say she is, or was, now with the FBI?"

"Yes, sir."

"Then why are we here?"

The others stared at him. These were the five most profound words they had ever heard him say.

"You are correct, Sir," said Gizmo. "It is the FBI's problem."

The chairman adjourned the panel with no conclusions for an indefinite period because the proper agency to address the issue was the FBI.

This was the second time the chairman understood things perfectly. He was becoming quite adept in this strange world.

The End

Will the team risk their necks for an enemy who comes to them with a warning? Mara, an untried member of the family, tests her training and resolve under threat in State of Nature. Find it at your favorite store: https://www.charlemagnefiles.com/linkmap.

Join the Charlemagne Files newsletter for more stories and information about the series, its world of covert operations, and the lives of the characters on the team. Sign up here: https://www.charlemagnefiles.com/contact.

If you enjoyed this book, please consider leaving a short review at your favorite bookstore.

GLOSSARY OF TERMS

AK-47 - developed by Mikhail Kalashnikov in 1947, one of the most ubiquitous firearms worldwide. It is reliable, uses standard 7.62 x 39mm ammunition, inexpensive and fully automatic. Pretty much standard issue for insurgents and terrorists everywhere.

Babysitter - a government officer or agent responsible for the care, feeding, and security of a specialist under contract to that government, as well as for the fulfillment of the contract.

Beretta - an Italian-made weapon by the oldest continuous manufacturer of firearms in the world.

Dangle - slang for an otherwise uninvolved person used as bait in an operation to trap a target.

Glock - semi-automatic pistol manufactured by an Austrian company.

HK - Heckler & Koch, German manufacturer of popular automatic weapons, especially submachine guns and assault rifles.

M-16 - 5.56 mm American military assault rifle.

Running point - a term used in military and business applications to designate the lead in an operation. In a specialist operation, the position requires stealth and silence in removing especially dangerous obstacles such as watchers and snipers.

SAS - Special Air Service, the special forces unit of the British Army founded in 1941.

SCIF - Sensitive Compartmented Information Facility, a secure facility used by American and British military, security, and intelligence service to process sensitive compartmented information.

SIG Sauer - a German Swiss firearms manufacturer.

Specialist - an outside operative used by a government in extremely sensitive situations in which death of the opponent is likely and/or desired.

Tango - military slang for a hostile operative, usually a terrorist.

touch - a listening tap.

tradecraft - a set of skills necessary for operating in a clandestine or intelligence-gathering environment.

www.ingramcontent.com/pod-product-compliance
Lightning Source LLC
Chambersburg PA
CBHW070522260626
47161CB00004B/1615